MW01235230

SHAND

Otis Aubert

Shand

Otisaubert.com

Copyright © 2016 Otis Aubert, Memphis

All rights reserved. No part of this book may be reprinted or reproduced or utilized in any form or by any electronic, mechanical, or other means, now know of hereafter invented, including photocopying and recording, or in information storage or retrieval systems, without permission in writing from the author.

ISBN: 978-1530200702

Table of Contents

CHAPTER I

The Native

It was early afternoon on the twenty-first day of his journey when Shand rowed through floating wreckage. The sea breeze was cooler than usual, moving fast and attacking with a stinging mist. Shand's fair skin did not agree with such conditions. His face was chapped and sore, his knuckles cracked and red. He tasted a hint of blood as he sniffed and breathed through a raw throat. His exhales were insulated beneath the pelts, heating his neck and chest.

Shand was a strong young man—more capable than most grown men. He stood slightly shorter than average, but he was dense and just as wide as a big man. He had a light green iris in his undamaged eye with an unusual amount of yellow highlights. His nose and cheeks were sprinkled with light freckles that complemented a thin auburn beard too new to even start the braid his tribesmen wore.

He adjusted the skins that wrapped his head to watch the beach with his good eye. The rocky shores and steep cliffs to which he was accustomed had disappeared two days ago, giving way to grey sand beaches gently sloping into dense, green forest.

Before long, he spotted cargo—crates and containers of all sorts. Some floated just off shore, being pulled and pushed by the surf. Others were partially sunken in the sand just beyond the tide. Wreckage was everywhere, but he saw no bodies, alive or dead.

For the remainder of the morning, he kept the boat just offshore, watching the beach and tree line. Shand did not need additional supplies, and he knew Uncle Royce would have his throat for even considering going ashore.

But Royce was not there, and Shand had never been much of a spectator.

After lightly beaching his rig, Shand grabbed his small axe and jumped down to the sand. It had been over a week since his last stop, and his land legs were unsure at best. He moved slowly while inspecting the mess, expecting to see something gruesome protruding from the sand or peeking out from under the piles of broken boards.

Shand wondered how large the vessel must have been. The boards were wider and longer than anything he had seen.

It must have been as big as a whale.

It must have taken ten rowers to move the monster.

He remembered the first time he'd heard of a spine and board boat. It had been the biggest news ever to hit his village. He remembered how excited his father was after seeing what he called a "plank boat" at sea, and the story of his father chasing the strange boat and its two backward-facing paddlers into a storm, only to lose them in the waves and nearly drown. He remembered the friendly competition among his village's fisherman to recreate the design and leave their primitive tree-hollowed boats in the past. It seemed to be the topic of every conversation: whose boat was looking the best, were oars really better than paddles, and if the boats

2

would even work at all. The fishermen would work late into the night, visiting one another's worksites to discuss new ideas and poke fun at each other's mistakes. This infused an energy into his tribe like never before. He remembered how everyone seemed brighter, taller. People spoke to each other in a friendlier way and seemed more willing to help one another. A sense of community was formed that had not been there before.

The crates were unopened, and Shand saw no tracks, so he relaxed a little and began popping open the boxes with his axe. Mostly, he saw what he expected—ceramic jugs and vases packed in straw, holding grain and water. His only unique find was a crate packed with jugs full of a clear, potent type of alcohol he had never smelled before.

I should not have stopped, he thought. A silly mistake I cannot take back.

On his hurried return to the boat, Shand realized he had left one crate unopened. He tried to ignore *the voice* in his head, persuading him in its raspy whisper to go back for the crate's unknown contents. *"You can't just leave the last one... There is only one more... You know you're going back. Might as well make it now, and quick."* Shand slowed to a stop "You're right," he grumbled.

Shand trotted back to the remaining box, fell to his knees and plunged his axe into a seam on the crate. Prying the boards apart, his eye caught a flash—a shimmer of gold through the straw. Shand tore the remaining boards away and began tossing straw. Each handful removed revealed a new color—deep purples and reds of fine clothes—bright greens and blues of gems seated in beautiful necklaces, ornate and heavy like the ones the elders from large tribes wore; and at the bottom, wrapped in heavy cloth, was a jeweled dagger and a beautifully made sword.

He had never seen such riches up close. He was surprised how much different they felt, how superior they were compared to what he was accustomed. These things had to belong to a very powerful person.

His mind began to race with the possibilities.

He could only begin to imagine the value.

It could change everything for his family. Maybe the entire village.

"Get on with it!"

Shand jerked the crate over his shoulder and hustled back to the boat. As he passed the cargo crates, he began to reconsider collecting the extra supplies. Grain and alcohol were always valuable trading goods, and he had the room.

"You're not going back, are you? You don't need extra supplies. You have treasure."

"I have to."

Shand was glad he had convinced Royce to build the boat so big, easily three horses long, eight hands above water, enough room to have a storage area and a small shelter in the hull. Shand had taken his time and a lot of pride in its construction, making sure everything was not only functional but also crafted to perfection and made from the best material known. The center of the deck was covered with a tented sheet of red fabric, waterproofed with Royce's special mixture of oil and beeswax. The

4

tent was open to the stern and bow. Both sloped sides of the tent were equipped with a roll-up window just above the oar cutout.

It was the biggest plank boat anyone in the village had attempted to build—so big, they were unsure if Shand would be able to row it effectively. Royce would chuckle to himself when carving the enormous oars, or after many other "best guess" decisions.

Shand would smile back, but always followed with: "She's built for distance, not for speed."

On his final trip, Shand bent over to grab the last of the alcohol and noticed some irregularities in the sand. He knew they weren't his own tracks, but couldn't quite figure them out. The tracks were spread out and messy, as if a wrestling match had taken place.

"Time to go."

As he followed the tracks, each disruption of the sand became clearer until a scene of what happened began to unfold in Shand's mind.

Frozen, Shand stared at perfect human handprint, realizing the tracks had been difficult to decipher because they were left by someone crawling to the forest.

Shand squinted, studying the tree line. He stroked his soft beard and listened, waiting for something to stand out against the leaves. The shadowed gaps between the trees began playing tricks on his eyes, becoming figures and shapes that he knew were not there. He could feel his imagination creeping up behind him.

"Time to go!"

He quickly carried his last load to the boat and prepared to depart.

Shand wanted to row away as fast as possible, but he didn't. He just stood and watched.

There could be a survivor, he thought. He could not just *leave*.

"You cannot be serious."

"I have to."

Shand thought about taking the new sword, but he hadn't met a man or beast that could match him with his small axe. "Little Man," he called it, weighted and shaped to perfection. The body of the axe was deer antler, about three hands long, on a slight continuous curve, with hide string weaved around the handle portion. Its bronze head was small enough for quick action, no bigger than his palm, and just soft enough to stave off breakage. His second favorite possession.

Shand hopped down and quickly made his way to the tree line. He did not hesitate. His focus came on quicker when given no time to ponder. As he strutted through the sand, his calves burned with each push, his breath catching his canter until he faced the edge of the forest; then with a deep breath he slid through the foliage and into the woods.

It was almost dark inside, the dim haze made worse by his eye adjusting to the lower light. He felt like he'd stepped into a dream, or into another world. The air was heavier, and the sounds inside were crisper, more complete. He listened closely and chose his steps carefully as the forest came into focus.

He smelled her first.

A flowered perfume mixed with her overripe personal scent.

He spotted her bare feet.

She was lying face-up, arms and legs spread.

Shand did not smell death, but maybe it was still new.

She wore fine clothing like that found in the treasure crate. Her face was still pink and full, both feet bare and bloody. She had a long thin nose and a strong chin, olive skin and deep brown hair—curly and thick.

She was beautiful.

He squatted next to her and poked her ribs with the axe.

She was still soft.

Placing his ear to her mouth, he listened...Nothing.

Shand was from Long Sky, a remote village on the east bank of the North Sea, where the proper way to honor the woman would be burning or burying her body. He thought the last thing he should do was make a fire to be seen for miles, but Shand wasn't one for digging either. He figured a shallow grave would suffice the gods, given his predicament.

It was almost pleasant under the forest canopy, much drier and even a bit warmer, which eased the torture of the dig. He hadn't seen anyone in over a week and felt a sense of company. She seemed peaceful, like she was napping under the sun in a meadow.

Shand imagined her life.

The life of opulence.

He took pride in his general objectiveness. However, the subject of *class* had deep personal grains, beginning in childhood and his first meeting with *the collectors*— finely dressed men from powerful tribes extorting furs and gold from Shand's village as payment for "protection" from other large tribes. He remembered how they would stand in the doorway, just far enough inside to convey dominance, just far enough out to claim courtesy. Their presence was an invasion of his home. A violation he would never forgive. As far back as he could remember, he had fantasized that the powerful were miserable people without direction, charred soulless demons with an unquenchable thirst for valueless shiny objects.

But he wanted to believe she was different, a beautiful angel, innocent and kind, oblivious to the moral crimes of her family.

Her fear and love must be human like mine, he thought.

Her perception just corrupted by a family whose souls were poisoned long ago.

He liked her. Her face seemed kind.

"Absurd! She's beautiful, silent, and you haven't seen anyone in weeks. She is no different from all the other thieves of labor. Just focus on digging and getting out of here."

Shand picked up the pace, chopping roots with his axe and shoveling with his hands.

He equated the acceptability of the grave to his fatigue, so it wasn't long before he was ready to roll her in.

He grabbed both ankles and gave a firm jerk to get her moving. But just as the body reached the end of the tug, she took a deep jolted breath, shocking Shand into stumbling and releasing her legs. She tried to rise, but her arms buckled, and her head returned to the ground like a dropped melon.

Her body tightened, raising rigid arms and legs into the air like an insect on its back.

Shand froze.

His breath stopped.

She wasn't breathing; everything was flexed and paralyzed. All he could do was stare. He had never seen a human body behave that way. Maybe that was her dying breath, he thought.

He could not move, only watch her animal-like body as it reached for the gods, asking to be taken. Not quite alive, not dead, somewhere in between.

Slowly, her body began to loosen. Her arms and legs slowly returned to drape the ground. She took a few quick gasps, then her breathing turned labored and gargled.

"Hello?" he called. Shand raised his voice. "What is your name?"

Still, no response.

Shand hurried back to the boat to get some food and water.

"Just leave! She's going to die either way."

When he returned, the woman's eyes were closed, and her breath was steadied and near silent again. Shand tilted her head and poured water over her lips. She attempted to swallow, then turned away and muttered something.

"What was that?" Shand asked.

"Brùid," she whispered. "Brùid."

Shand did not understand. He tried to get the woman to drink again, but to no avail.

"What are you saying? Hello?"

Shand lifted the woman's head and placed it in his lap. He pushed her feet together, adjusting the dress to better cover her legs, then rested her hands across her stomach. He wanted to end her misery, to pull her up, hand over fist from the mire of dying—to rescue her.

But Shand was no healer, and had no experience with the injured or the dying. The older villagers always handled those matters.

Shaking her awake ended in failure, of course, along with slapping her alive.

Feeling stupid and helpless, he convinced himself she was too far-gone, and he should just comfort her.

Shand stroked her hair and began telling her stories from his life, beginning with his oldest and most favorite memory—his first boat trip. He told her the freedom he had felt on that first trip anchored deep inside him, never to leave. He told her how he felt guilty about not being a better son and brother.

He spoke to her as if he was confessing to the gods. He felt maybe she could return, following the path of truthful words, and maybe he could be healed with his confessions.

He talked until he bored himself, asking a question every so often, just in case.

The sun was getting low, so he slipped out from beneath her head to gather sticks and cut bark for a small fire. Shand was the master of fire, or at least he thought so. He had never failed to get an ember. Uncle Royce always delegated the fire making to Shand, even in the presence of adults and Shand's father. Maybe it was intentional, just to rib the others, or maybe it was to push Shand. Either way, he could make fire quicker than anyone he knew.

Shand got the blaze going just in time to head off the insect invasion. The labor drained the last bit of energy that he had for the day. He rested his back against a tree and removed his sheepskin boots to dry by the fire. His eyes were heavy, and he could feel the fatigue setting in deeper with each yawn. Sliding down from the tree and onto his side, he stretched out close to the fire, resting his head on his folded arm.

He watched the woman's still body and smooth face flicker in the firelight as the forest grew dark, his sympathy slowly consumed by gratefulness that he did not share her condition.

Shand awoke with a jerk to noise on the beach. It was still dark, but with a hint of morning glow. Quietly, he gathered himself and made his way to the tree line.

The sounds were voices.

Of many.

Silhouetted figures walking on the beach, dragging wreckage and climbing on his boat, speaking a language he had never heard. Short and choppy, like barking.

The sun would be up shortly and he knew they would see his tracks.

He needed to get to safety immediately.

But the woman was still alive and he didn't want to *simply* leave her, especially if the people on the beach were those soulless savages from his village's stories— tales of cannibalistic tribes he heard since childhood and since tried to forget.

They were probably the woman's people returning for their goods and any survivors. Maybe he could explain the situation to her civilized people. Surely they would understand and see how he tried to care for the woman. But maybe their punishment would be even worse than the cannibals'?

Shand knelt behind a tree and anxiously waited for the light, thinking about what a stupid mistake he had made, and how Royce might handle the situation.

"There is nothing to see. It doesn't make a difference either way, just go!"

Slowly, the figures became clearer until he could see that their faces were tattooed with intricate dotted designs, and they wore the bowl-shaped haircuts he recalled from the stories. Their small bodies moved quick and jerky under thick skins draping their shoulders.

Shand couldn't believe the stories were true. They looked so different than in his imagination. Most had hair like the sun, yellow and glowing, and their skin was light and milky with a slight glow of its own, almost opposite from the tiny-headed thick-necked savages his mind had conjured.

Shand hustled back to the woman, paused, and surveyed the area. Spotting a large rock, he pried it out of the ground, then lifted it above his head. He wobbled over to the woman, his arms quivering under the weight, his heart a drum.

His mouth was noisy with deep breaths sucking through excessive saliva. A desperate madness began to boil as he stood over the woman, staring at her face. He imagined the rock crushing her skull, the sounds it would make, the mess it might create, and the fact it might take more than once.

"Hurry! Get it over with!"

"I can't."

Shand tossed the rock away, then sat next to the woman. He pulled her into his lap and wrapped his arm around her neck. Strong and tight he pulled her in—long enough to make sure.

Shand covered the body with brush, then hurried into the forest, heading south along the tree line, attempting to cover his tracks as he went. He slipped and cussed over the rocks and mud as he tried climbing high on the hill in order to keep his boat in sight. He made a final scramble to ascend a rock shelf, just in time to watch his boat be officially stolen. His chest tightened, and his face warmed with anger as he watched the little natives board his boat along with a few of their small tree-hollowed boats. He wished he could storm his boat, cracking heads and severing limbs in a firestorm of rage upon the little demons.

"Calm down, there is nothing you can do."

Shand took a deep breath and tried to run through his options. Maybe their village was right around the bend. Maybe he could find tracks.

As Shand began his descent, he caught movement on the beach from the corner of his eye.

A native remained, standing still and staring over Shand's tracks.

Bent down, the little native calmly ran his fingers through the sand, looking stone-faced towards Shand's camp, then slowly gathered a few things that Shand could not identify and packed them into a sack. He strapped the sack to his back, and in no hurry, walked along Shand's tracks and disappeared into the forest.

"You know you can't allow yourself to be hunted."

"I know," Shand grunted.

Shand stayed as high on the hill as he could while making his way back, walking slowly and trying to keep quiet, stopping frequently to give a good listen and watch the forest.

He began hearing sounds he could not identify from all directions.

Shand grew anxious.

I should have brought Thief, he thought. That little savage would have been sniffed out long ago.

Shand squatted under the cover of a small tree. He held his breath and scanned the forest inch by inch, listening, and staring so hard that his focus blurred.

Too much time had passed.

"Just get out of here!"

His only chance now was tracking the native from the beach, which could pose a problem. He had spent much more time fishing than hunting.

He trotted diagonally down the ridge, his anxiousness growing into anger, his thoughts fixed on getting his hands on the little native.

Just as Shand hopped over a fallen tree, he heard a fast whistle, then felt a sharp punch in his left side below the ribs. As he landed, his knees buckled, crashing him into a thorny bush.

"He got you."

Anticipating an immediate onslaught, Shand fought through the thicket as fast as he could in hopes of retaining an adequate defensive position.

As he ripped through the thorny vines, he saw movement from behind the trees. Shand knelt, peeking over the fallen tree trunk. He watched, frozen, trying to regulate his breathing and assess the damage. The movement was no doubt the native, and he wasn't trying to hide. He was small and skinny, draped in a fur shawl made from white and grey rabbit pelts. He casually walked, appearing then disappearing behind the trees not five horses away, his bright green eyes never looking in Shand's direction. He was picking up sticks, inspecting them, then tossing them back.

Shand kept half his eye on the wandering native as he inspected his wound. The spear had been plucked out during his tumble, and hadn't penetrated too deep.

"That's the last mistake this savage will make!"

Shand's ears burned. His chest swelled.

"Hey!" Shand called. "I'm going to chop your little round head off!"

The native did not respond, or even look up from his stick inspection. He was relaxed to the point of oddness, which injected a sliver of doubt into Shand's courage.

The little savage must have found a stick he liked, because he squatted and started to fiddle with it.

Shand was obviously more powerful than the older, smaller native, and thought he must be a fool for keeping such a short distance.

Shand ripped off his right sleeve, then tore the sleeve into long strips. He dressed his wound with the strips, trying to calm himself and think logically. But his emotions would not let his mind take control. He could feel the warm rage spread through his veins, and truthfully, he could have tried harder to maintain rationale, but it felt good, and he welcomed it. There was no voice trying to convince him to resist this time. Both were in agreement on submission to the rising fury.

Shand chipped a slab of bark from a tree, then tied it around his left forearm with some of the sleeve strips.

"Good idea. This little bowl-headed demon is in big trouble."

Leading with his barked arm held high, Shand advanced, keeping his left foot forward with his right arm gripping Little Man, hanging low in the rear.

The native remained still until Shand cut the distance by a third.

Then he stood and walked away.

Shand charged, keeping Little Man hanging back, protected, to be revealed just before the strike.

The native matched, then surpassed Shand's stride, cutting back and forth through the trees like a deer. Realizing the native was much more agile, and not to waste valuable energy, Shand cut the chase short. A brief thought of throwing the axe crossed his mind, but he did not want to die a fool.

Kneeling behind a tree, Shand rested and watched the native stroll back to the same safe distance, then squat and return to carving his next spear. Shand held still, catching his breath and staring at the native's face, trying to see his eyes.

When Shand was a boy, a fishing accident left him with a dead eye on his right side—grey and cloudy with a scar just off-center. He wanted the native to look up and see his demon eye. The eye he used to scare children and awaken insecurity in adults. But of course the little savage paid no attention. He stayed hunched, looking down, patiently whittling his stick.

As Shand's heart slowed, a sense of doom washed over him.

The forest seemed to close in around him.

He felt like trapped prey.

Panic began to set in.

Before Shand could think, his body jumped up and ran. He knew he should stop, but he could not control himself. His legs just kept pumping as he waited for the spear to pierce his back. He slipped through trees the best his stout frame would allow, trying to keep the straightest line possible, putting as many trees as he could between himself and the native.

Over ridges and through ravines, he clipped along at a pace that surprised him. But the effort shortly began to strangle his lungs and turn his stomach ablaze. Shand knew if he did not slow down, he would be too tired to defend himself if struck, so he darted behind a tree to look back.

Shand held his breath and listened, scanning each tree trunk for irregular shapes peeking out from behind. He held perfectly still, waiting for a crackle of sticks, or for a quick shadow to appear at the corner of his eye. He breathed low and slow, trying to idle his thumping heart. It was difficult to remain still and quiet. His legs were painfully weak, quivering beyond his control, his stomach sick and hollow, and his organs felt like they were suffocating. A cold sensation began to drain from behind his heart, then climbed into his veins, causing the hair to stand up on his neck and scalp.

No longer human. He was a hunted rabbit—hyper-focused, painfully alert.

He could almost feel his rabbit ears twitching at the forest noises.

"Be patient. Don't move 'til you're sure."

He could smell the dirt and taste the wet leaves in the air. His senses had never been so sharp, acute to the point of irritated. He tried to settle and remain calm as he waited for the shock to recede and for reason to return. But the instinct had a mind of its own, holding Shand fast in his heightened state, wanting to decide for itself when things were safe. Shand's fingertips gripped the bark. His eye bounced back and forth from trunk to trunk like a hawk's.

Patient and still, he listened to the forest in incredible detail, the birdcalls and insect noises deeply layered, creating an ocean of sound, complex, yet somehow simple and beautiful. He breathed deeply, inhaling the forest and exhaling the panic. Little by little his heart began to slow. His hawk eye relaxed, and his strangled insides began to loosen.

He'd lost him.

Shand thought the native must have cut his losses or fallen.

He began to feel the overwhelming excitement one can only experience after escaping death. The kind that makes you feel born again.

Rejuvenated, he headed for higher ground to resume his hunt. His wound was burning but not bleeding too much, and he felt strong.

He had only made it halfway up the hill when he heard that familiar whistle. Shand tried to take cover, but he was too slow. The moment Shand began his dive, his ear was struck with a painful glancing blow.

"There goes your ear."

Shand scrounged on hands and knees to press his body against a tree that he thought was in between him and the native. His head swiveled back and forth like a bird checking its flanks.

Seeing only forest and hearing only birds, he slowly peeked from behind the tree.

"That's a good way to lose your other eye! Dash away and spot him on the run."

But just as Shand was about to act on the advice, he spotted the native up the hill, perched on a rock, calm and casual as usual. He was squatted, balanced on the balls of his feet with his arms hanging over his knees.

The native jumped down and began searching the forest floor for more worthy branches. He kicked and shuffled the leaves like a child, humming and whistling every so often.

Shand knew the native would never give a second thought about killing him. His worth was equal only to the thrill of the kill, a trophy, a story to be bragged about, and maybe a fireside tale warning children of the red-haired beast-men of the forest. He was nothing to this savage, simply a challenge, a stimulation soon to be erased from existence. It brought on a feeling of liberation in Shand—a freedom from empathy.

Shand began a search too, but he was searching for a perfect spot. He gathered a few limbs for himself, thinking that maybe he would give the native a taste of his own medicine.

The native followed Shand at his familiar distance, humming and making clicking noises. He began to tease Shand with quick shuffles of his feet or a projected grunt. Anything to give Shand's heart a jump. It was like being stalked by his younger sister. He couldn't believe this little devil had him in such a predicament.

Before long, Shand turned and sat in a small clearing. The native stopped too, crouched, and returned to whittling. Shand matched the native with some whittling of his own. He watched the native's bowl-cut blonde hair wiggle and sway as he worked—no emotion, no eye contact.

After the savage finished two spears, he stood. Shand quickly stood too, positioning himself behind a large oak. The native began walking in a circle around Shand, in and out of trees as Shand rotated around his. The native began jumping and darting, looking for an open angle. Shand would fake throw his spear in response, attempting to disrupt the native's attack. Shand must have made twenty rotations before the savage faked his usual move, then cut back, throwing the spear with his left hand. It was a weaker throw but still found the edge of Shand's thigh. Not strong enough to stick but good enough to do damage. The native missed with his second throw, too excited with his prior hit.

As the day passed, the scene was repeated again and again. Sometimes the native would take his time. Other times he would rush in, throwing both spears back to back. Shand was getting good at dodging spears. He was most proud of correctly anticipating the throw, and he even tried to catch a few.

Shand had been hit three times with minimal damage before the native finally sat and rested against a tree.

This time, the native did not whittle or ignore Shand. He sat still, staring at Shand the same way Shand had been trying to find the native's eyes earlier.

The native wore a look of contempt, and his body language reflected agitation. He was not having fun anymore.

Shand did not ignore the native like the native had done to him. He stared back, directly into the native's eyes, holding his gaze until the native looked away. Tired and slouching, the native would yawn and stretch, then pretend to be interested in some faraway noise, or pick at his feet for a while, but he would always return to lock eyes with Shand. Sometimes only briefly, other times for minutes. Shand felt he could almost hear what the native was thinking, or, more so, feeling.

A mischievous smirk grew on the native's mouth every so often, like a thought of doing something monstrous to Shand was passing behind his eyes. Every slight expression change or movement the native made began to tell a horror story, at least in Shand's mind.

The staring contest reminded Shand of when he would look into an animal's eyes, trying to identify something with which he could make a connection, but would always come up short.

Sitting quietly, they each watched the other's face slowly fade into the shadows of evening, while the woods took on a new and louder song, its volume gradually increasing until the forest became endless chambers of pulsating sounds, a trance-inducing symphony that struck a chord of *smallness* in Shand. It reminded him of childhood, when he would look beyond the fire during story time, into the depths of the forest, listening to the stories of heroes and superstitions and wondering himself into a dream.

Shand soon lost sight of the native in the dark, only hearing his occasional movements mixed with some sniffing and breathing.

Before long, he heard the native stand and take steps. Shand's senses perked, and he readied himself for an attack. But the steps began moving away, quieter and quieter in the distance until they were gone.

Shand removed his cloth pants and began cutting the bottom portions into thin strips.

It was a few hours before he heard the first faint crackle of sticks. Then another, and another. Shand laid perfectly still.

Again and again, the soft snaps of sticks—failed attempts at stepping lightly—became louder and clearer, until he knew the native was back. The native spotted Shand lying motionless, arms crooked and uncomfortable, giving the impression of incapacitation or death. The native knelt and waited, watching Shand for signs of life.

Shand remained still.

The native quietly took a step closer, then again.

Still, no movement.

The native raised his spear and took another step. Now he was half the distance he usually kept. Still no movement from Shand. The native slowly took aim, then launched a spear. It whistled through the trees and stuck in Shand's midsection.

Still no movement.

The native held still, watching and listening.

Nothing.

He gripped the remaining spear with both hands and moved forward, increasing his speed with each step, accelerating to the perfect velocity for a glorious piercing of Shand's heart.

Just as he reached speed and was almost upon him, Shand pulled the strip of pant that triggered the snare, snatching one of the native's legs into the air, but not as high as Shand had hoped. The native jumped around, hopping on one leg and trying to get the snare off the other. Shand immediately dug himself out from the hole he had dug, the hole that had hidden his body from knees to neck, covered with layers of soil and bark he used as a replacement body.

He charged the native, tackling him and pulling his snared leg towards the ground. The native yelled in pain, then in rage as he squirmed and tried to bite Shand's neck and face.

He was surprisingly strong for his size, and as slippery as oil.

He would have been long gone if not for the snare.

Each time he slipped Shand's grip, the native did not have enough time to remove the snare before Shand tackled him, landing on top of the native with all his weight, pushing out a little more strength from the native's body each time.

The native fought like an animal, spitting and biting, head-butting and scratching.

No breaks to catch breath or regain strength.

Just unhinged ferocity.

There would be no *giving up*.

He would fight as long as his body would allow.

Shand was completely wet with sweat before his weight and size were too much for the native. The little savage finally went limp, lying on his back, his left leg elevated, hanging from the snare.

Shand quickly gathered some extra strips, then flipped the native over and tied his hands behind his back. He cut the snare, then tied his ankles together. To complete the capture, he tied the savage's wrist-binding to his ankle-binding.

The native did not move or struggle. He said nothing and made no noises.

Shand searched the native's sack to find a bladder of fresh water and some dried roots that smelled like feet. He couldn't help but drink too much of the water. It sat heavy and uneasy on an empty stomach. After taking some test nibbles from the roots, he packed everything back in the native's sack and sat to rest. The sun would be up soon and Shand needed sleep if he would be worth anything tomorrow. He tied the native's bindings to a vine, then to a tree. He also tied another vine around the native's neck, then to a second tree, thinking he would surely hear if the native tried to get out of that mess.

Shand sat and leaned his back against a tree to ensure his sleep would not be too deep. He adjusted his skins to try and cover any insect entryways, then closed his eyes and tried to think of something other than his boat. The native remained still, not twitching with bug bites or trying to reposition. Shand thought the native must have some remedy for the mosquitos, or maybe his pungent odor kept them away.

Shand awoke to sunlight peeking through an opening between the skins, one of a hundred rays scattered by the forest, extracting moisture from the plants and steaming the woods with a warm, light haze.

Shand unwrapped the skins from his head and wiped the sleep from his eyes. His neck and back were tight from sleeping upright all night, and it took some extra stretches and cracks to get him straight.

He crawled over to the hog-tied native and cut the strip connecting the wrist knots to his ankle knots, then untied his wrist binding from behind his back and retied them in front. The native did not try to resist. Even when his hands were free, he remained submissive and calm, looking at the ground, and letting Shand move and position his limbs freely.

Shand raised him to a sitting position, then took a stick and drew his boat in the dirt. The drawing was crude, but was sure to be understood. He pointed at the boat with the stick, then pointed south and remained still, staring at the native.

The native did not move, looking uninterested.

Shand raised the stick in the air.

The native turned away, expecting to be struck, but Shand lowered the stick and pointed at the boat again, then south.

Still no response.

Shand struck the native across the neck with a quick whip of the stick. The native tucked his chin and fell, attempting to protect his face and neck with his shoulder. Shand gripped the native's neck and raised him back up, then forced his head down above the image.

Again, he pointed at the boat, then south.

The native remained still and silent.

Shand raised the stick again.

The native took a breath and braced for the strike. This time Shand hit him twice with all his force.

Again, the native fell, squirming in pain on the ground. Shand stood over the native, threatening another strike, waiting for a response. But the native said nothing and gave no signs. Shand began hitting the native across the head and neck with the stick. The native rolled and jerked around, groaning and whining, trying to cover his head and face with his hands as Shand pushed and stomped them away. With each strike, the skin on the native's head and hands became more swollen and tight, until finally splitting open and creating a bloody, hairy mess.

Shand couldn't believe he had gotten nothing from the native. He began to feel unsure and guilty.

"He knows exactly what you're saying. Don't let him gain control."

Shand did not know what else to do, and agreed he could not be made a fool of, so the beating continued, having to switch striking arms every so often to share the fatigue.

The native's body language began to change, and he started to grab at the stick and Shand's legs. It was clear that these attempts were futile, and must have just been a last push, because shortly after, he spoke. Shand did not understand him, but it was a sign, and Shand felt relieved. He put the stick down and wiped the native's bloody lips with a pant strip.

"Batur, batur," the native repeated.

Shand retrieved the stick and began scanning the forest with it, moving it slowly along the arc of an invisible circle surrounding them.

When the point reached an almost perpendicular angle to the coast, the native urgently grunted. Shand raised the native to his feet, cut the ties between his ankles, and tightened the ones between his wrists. He tied a thin vine to the wrist-binding to use as a leash, then poked him in the direction the native had indicated.

Deliberate with each step, the native slowly stepped through the forest, careful not to fall with tied hands. Too careful, really; like he was putting on a show. He even faked a few slips, then held his wrist-binding out for

Shand to see the problem. But the native was a horrible actor, and Shand was having none of it.

Shand did not have to strike the native to have him return to pace, just threaten to. He had established his diligence, and there would be no benefit for the native to test Shand's patience.

From then on, the native held speed, even seeming to push the pace a bit, quickly pulling himself up ridges or sliding and hopping down ravines, almost pulling the leash from Shand's hand. Shand had to jerk the native the way you would a horse to keep him under control.

Shand felt they had kept with the original direction, but he couldn't be positive. The deeper into the forest they went, the denser the foliage became, and the more difficult it was to keep his sense of direction.

It wasn't long before Shand's hefty body was wet with sweat and becoming weak. He knew the native could hear him breathe harder and step heavier, so he poked the native in the back and signaled for a stop. He pulled the native to the ground by his wrist bindings, using his left hand; his right hand he kept back, gripping the axe. He then rolled the native on to his side and tied his feet together.

The native struggled after he realized Shand was not untying his hands to be free, but to be retied behind his back again. Showing protest more than revolt, the native flexed, staring stone-faced at the ground. Shand pulled and tugged the native's arms. The native stiffened and moved his arms around, making it impossible for Shand to get the job done with one hand.

Finally, Shand rolled the native onto his stomach and put his knee on the back of the native's neck. He gradually rested more and more weight on the native's neck until he relaxed. Shand stuck Little Man into the dirt and retied the native's hands, then he sat against a tree to catch his breath.

The native rolled onto his side, then inched over to sit against a fallen tree. He stared at Shand with a dead face, as if it was made of clay. He remained perfectly still, only moving his eyes to follow Shand. Shand could feel the native staring, but he ignored him. He wanted to giggle at the native, as though his five-year-old brother was trying to scare him with a demon face.

When Shand began the fire stack, he noticed the native's eyes were fixed, staring into the forest. His pupils were large, and his mouth hung open.

Shand had never been one to succumb to superstition, but he couldn't help thinking of the spirits the native could be summoning in his trance. Spirits so dark and gruesome they were beyond imagination. The ones you could not see, only feel as they crawled in to leech your spirit.

Suddenly, the native gave out a deep bellow. "Oooohhhh...Oooohhh!"

"Ahhhh!" Shand yelled, scampering to prepare for the spirits.

The native began to convulse and yell louder, "Oooohhh!—Oooohhh!—Oooohhh!"

He rolled and jerked around on the ground like something was trying to get out of his body. Shand began stomping and kicking the native, yelling at him to stop. But the native kept flexing his body back and forth, screaming and projecting deep groans as if he were trying to expunge a sickness from his bowels.

A chill raised the hair on Shand's arms and neck. He wanted to smash the native's head into silence.

"Choke him!"

Not wanting his arms too close to the native's mouth, Shand ran to the supplies and grabbed a pant strip thick enough not to cut into the neck. But just as Shand turned to make his way back, he noticed the native trying to covertly slide his tied wrists under his butt with each flex.

"That little demon! Beat him even worse this time."

Shand calmly put the strip down and walked over to the native. He crouched beside the native's face and slowly pulled the stick from his waist, holding it still just above the native. Once the native caught a glimpse of the stick and pretended he didn't, Shand rolled him onto his back and laid on top of him. He grabbed the back of the native's neck and pulled his head in, forcing his chin to his chest. Then, with his other hand, Shand tried to force the end of the stick up the native's nose.

Even with tied hands behind his back, the native put up a good fight, contorting and sliding around, head-butting and biting. It took almost all Shand had left to keep the native underneath him while trying to position the stick.

After the first good *crunch*, the native went loose. Shand released his head to hit the ground like a rock. Blood streamed from the violated nostril. His eyes were closed, swollen and tearful, his breath fast and deep.

"This little savage is crazy."

"I know."

They rested side by side, breathing heavily and peeking at one another every so often.

Shand began to chuckle. A feeling of joy swept over him he could not explain. The native and his wildness had become hilarious to Shand.

The *giggles* hadn't infected Shand since he was a child, and it reminded him of laying in the dark after bedtime, laughing into the night with his younger brother Baird about silly things only they could fully understand. He began opening his eyes wide and pushing his face out at the native, giggling and waving his head, then giving grunts like the native: "Oohhh! Ooohhh!

It became more and more hilarious as he went. Louder and louder he giggled and *ooohhhed,* dancing around like he was losing his mind.

The native remained still, watching Shand from the corner of his eye, not sure exactly what was happening.

Shand's high peaked with a leaping kick crashing into a summersault, ending with Shand staring up into the trees with arms and legs spread.

He took a deep breath and a long exhale as the forest's canopy began playing tricks on his eyes— moving around like it was unhinged from the rest of the forest. The light shining through the leaves would expand to saturation, engulfing the forest and Shand's eye in a blonde blindness, then contract as the sun moved behind a cloud, extracting all color and leaving the forest in grey hues.

He felt like he had been drinking alcohol, but clean of the fog that accompanied drunkenness. He relaxed, watching the mirages and enjoying the calmness produced by the release. A light chuckle arose every so often, pushing out a puff of air and reminding Shand that he had a body. He couldn't remember the last time he'd felt so good.

Shand slowly rolled over to the native, still smiling and trying to hold back the giggles, like he was sneak-attacking Thief. He wiped the blood from the native's mouth and face and stuffed a little cloth in the nostril, then lifted the native to sit against the fallen tree.

Shand pulled the native's sack over to take inventory: Six medium-sized roots. A type of onion. A half-full bladder of water.

Shand cut one of the roots into bite-sized pieces, stabbed a piece with his stick and offered it to his captive. Without hesitation, the native leaned over and bit off the piece.

Shand couldn't help but feel a kinship with the native. No matter that neither man's life meant much to the other, they were sharing an extraordinary experience that no one else could understand. He began to feel a sense of respect for the native. A relationship had formed; regardless of its nature, good or bad, it existed, and therefore he felt it should be recognized.

"Ridiculous! Did you feel this way when he was in control? Do you think he did? He would cut your head off and take your children as slaves if he could!"

Shand took a deep breath and tried to refocus while they ate.

One piece for the native.
Two pieces for Shand.
One piece for the Native.
Three pieces for Shand.

Shand repeated this pattern until two roots were gone, and his stomach felt almost satisfied. After a few sips of water each, Shand hog-tied the native, then connected a vine from a tree to his neck like before.

Shand's belly no longer burned with hunger. He felt good and heavy, and he knew he would sleep deeply, so he tossed a pile of dead leaves on the native for an additional alert if the native moved.

That night was much quieter than usual, like the forest was a reflection of Shand's emotional and mental state. When he was stressed and alert, the forest had been alive and calling out, like it was rallying in support for Shand's cause; and now that he was calm, the forest rested.

As he drifted into sleep, he thought about the connection among all things, and how the forest might not be reflecting Shand's emotions or supporting his cause, but maybe it was being called to alarm in response to him, the unconnected intruder, letting the natives and everything else know where he was and in what condition.

In the morning, Shand felt terrible. There was twisting in his guts accompanied by sharp pains and sweating. "Stinky root made me sick!" Forcefully, he nudged the native awake with his foot. Ill and irritated, Shand tossed the bladder to the native, hitting him in the head, then pulled and jerked the native's ankle knots loose.

Shand picked the bladder off the ground and squirted two large sips into the native's mouth, then poked him forward, the same as before. Both were moving slower today, but Shand was definitely in worse shape. He was no longer paying attention to direction, but concentrated on keeping pace and pushing through his discomfort, trying to hide his weakness.

Near midday, he noticed a change. The forest appeared less dense. At a closer look, he realized they were on an obscure trail.

He immediately stopped the native.

But it was too late.

The native gave out a high-pitched yell.

Shand smacked the native across the neck, dropping him, but he continued to yell. Shand panicked and began beating him, but he just yelled louder. Grabbing some strips, he straddled the native and tried shoving the cloths in the native's mouth. Every time the native would yell, Shand would try to force the cloth in. That reduced the amount of noise, but Shand's fingers were too close to being bitten off, so he started using his stick to push the cloth into the corners of the native's mouth. Back and forth the native thrashed his head, yelling and choking while Shand stabbed and poked, scraping and gouging the native's face, until finally the native surrendered and let Shand fill his mouth with the cloth.

Shand was confident the native would not have called out unless he was sure to be heard, and figured there was a short time before whomever the savage had been calling would arrive. He thought about taking the native as a hostage, so he would have negotiating power, but quickly discarded that thought, knowing the natives did not value life as he did.

Thinking it would take a while for the native to work the packed cloth out of his mouth with tied hands, Shand bound the native's ankles together, then rolled him off the path into a small ravine.

Shand ran down the path in the same direction they had been headed, thinking he should cover as much ground as he could before hiding in the forest and letting the search party pass. Maybe he could let them pass, then follow their tracks back to their village before they made the round trip. Of course, he knew they could be coming from anywhere, but he felt it was the only chance he had.

After deciding he had covered enough ground, he left the path and headed into the woods.

Crouching behind a fallen tree, he watched the path and listened carefully. He wondered if he had left the path too soon, if maybe the native was already free, soon to meet his friends and hunt Shand down. Or maybe they would retrieve the native from a different path, and Shand would wait too long, sitting and waiting to be killed like oblivious prey.

Just as Shand considered heading farther into the forest, he heard the native's high-pitched yell. It echoed through the forest clean and fast, shooting though Shand's body like a bolt of lightning. He could tell the call came from near where Shand had left the native.

Over and over, the native yelled. With every shriek, Shand's heart beat faster. Again and again, the same yell, the same tone, the same duration. He could feel each yell climb the rungs of his spine until it reached the base of his skull, then turn to ice water and empty into his scalp, sending chills throughout his body, and standing all his hair on end.

Just when Shand thought he might lose control again, he heard another yell from the opposite direction, short and deep, and much closer than the native's call.

Shand froze, digging his fingers into the dirt.

"This is it. Be calm and quiet."

The first one to appear through the trees was the caller. Tall and thin, barking his call upwards into the forest like he was throwing it out of his mouth with a flick of his long neck. Shand's body tightened, his sights fixed.

One by one they passed, one tall, two short, another fat. Shand's mind began to race. He could control his body, but his thoughts were loose, fast and scattered. He couldn't help but think of their lives, children, and wives. He wondered whether the fat one was ridiculed like he would be in Shand's village—or was he revered and perceived as powerful? He imagined the natives eating body parts and feeding them to their children. He imagined them around the fire at night, telling stories of ghosts, demons, and other untruths, ensuring that their offspring stay primitive.

After they passed and the searcher's call was far enough away, Shand quickly headed down the path from where they'd come. He tried keeping a pace he could manage for a long period, breathing evenly, not running too fast.

The trail soon began a perpetual descent. The lower it led, the clearer and wider it became, until he knew he was getting close, so he slowed and quieted his pace.

Hearing the village before he saw it, Shand left the path and slowly made his way through the forest to find a good vantage point. He could hear women talking and children playing. There were stone-and-thatch dwellings bordering the village; he used those as cover while making his way around. He saw women sitting by small fires, talking and tending to stretched skins. He watched children chase chickens with sticks, yelling and laughing themselves into a frenzy.

"These are not humans—some sort of wild demon animals."

Shand came to a clearing on the far side of the village that was planted with small gardens in raised beds. As he scanned the clearing, he spotted a river peeking out from behind the tall grass with boats along its bank.

There it was.

The beautiful red tent of his favorite possession.

CHAPTER II

The Escape

Shand's stomach dropped. He wanted to sprint to his boat and row away as fast as he could, but he knew that would not be wise. He saw no men in the village, but that was not to say they weren't close by. He didn't have much time before the searchers would return, and he needed to make a decision quickly.

As Shand's mind raced through his options, he stared at his beautiful boat; he didn't know why, but he thought he should give it a name. Compared to the natives' small tree hollowed boats, his was like a work of art, carefully crafted with passion and precision. It must be a valuable prize for the village.

Shand figured his best option was to make his way up the river through the forest and find a secluded spot to slip into the water. Then he could wade back down and board his boat from behind.

He could not find any reeds that would be acceptable breathing sticks, so he gathered some vines and brush on his way up the river. He found a perfect spot to slip into the water undercover, hidden from any unknown eyes down the bank or across the river.

He shaped the vines into a crude bowl, then intertwined the brush around it. He threw the leftover foliage into the river, removed the water bladder and some roots from the native's sack and tucked them into his clothes, then slid down the bank and into the river.

The water was brown and the mud smelled like dung. The streams and rivers of his homeland were as clear as ice with rock bottoms, clean enough to drink. He couldn't wait to get away from this rancid land, never to see these dirty little natives again. His throat swelled and his eyes began to tear. He missed home like never before. He tried to push them aside, but images of his homeland floated uncontrollably in his mind. His favorite lake— perfectly still and reflecting the sky with absolute precision—and the secret peak he visited to get away from everything and watch the hawks. He could almost smell his home and feel his family's presence. He had thought he was unable to feel homesickness, but he was wrong.

Shand submerged his body to his neck, and then placed the stick bowl upside down over his head. He was afraid his clothes would become too heavy, so he stayed just outside the current and close enough to touch.

As Shand waded downriver, he tried to mimic the speed of the brush piles he'd thrown into the current earlier to keep a natural pace and not draw any attention.

As Shand and the bowl danced down the river, he watched a shattered image of the bank, ever-changing as the bowl turned and bobbed in the current. He watched turtles perched on logs as he passed by, none giving a single look in Shand's direction. He felt invisible, like the cats from his village stalking in tall grass. It was almost loud under the bowl, his breathing trapped and amplified, interrupted only by his spits of water.

Approaching the clearing, he could see children playing on the bank. They were grouped off, throwing dull spears at each other, none with the slightest interest in what was floating in the river.

Even the native children put a fright into Shand. Big-headed, little-bodied, translucent-like beasts, mostly communicating in strange jerky gestures. Violence was their true language. The bloodthirst was visible in the youngest of them, unlocked and nurtured from the beginning.

Shand floated behind the row of boats, not removing the stick bowl until he reached his boat. Carefully, he pulled out Little Man and hooked him over the boat's edge. Leaving his lower half loose, he pulled himself up and quietly slid over the side like a snake.

Shand stayed low, crawling around and taking inventory. The boat had been almost completely unloaded except for the jugs of alcohol, some scattered rations, and a few pieces of clothing. Slowly, Shand unfastened the port side oar. He crawled to the bow and sawed through the rope anchoring the boat, then quietly lowered it into the river. He leaned over the side and used the oar to try and push off. Slightly exposed, he watched the children, waiting for one of them to look in his direction and cry out. The boat was more grounded than Shand had thought, and just pushing with the oar was not enough. He began to feel that familiar rush of panic rising from his guts. Without thinking, he grabbed the bow and began jerking his body back and forth.

"Relax, you fool! Your impatience is like a child's. There's no need to rush."

Shand jumped, looking back. The voice came from behind his left ear instead of from inside his head as usual; it was louder than normal and more distinctive, less like a whisper and more like a village elder. Shand stayed frozen. His hands squeezed the sides of the boat as he peered over his shoulder, waiting for the voice to appear in whatever unimaginable form was the most horrifying.

"Hello?" Shand whispered. "Hello?"

Shand had heard *the voice* for the first time around a year ago. It began as a quiet thought, a suggestion from his conscience with no real voice, just his own guilt or intuition making its opinions clear. But with each suggestion or request, *the voice* grew into something Shand could hear, but only in his mind.

Shand gave a strong jerk and felt the boat loosen.

He quickly knelt back down, watching for reactions as he began to float away.

Surprisingly, he was halfway out of sight before one of the children looked his way. The child watched for a moment, then pointed.

One of the older boys yelled something at the group, then headed towards the bank. A few children stopped playing to watch. The older boy smacked and kicked away a couple of younger, over-energized boys trying to tag along.

As Shand rounded the bend, he watched the older boy slowly pull the cut rope from the water, hand over fist until he reached the severed end. Shand knew he had made a big mistake. Now there was no perceived accident, and the chase would soon be on.

His only chance was making it to the coast; if he was out of sight by the time his pursuers got there, then they would not know which way he went.

After Shand rounded the bend, he quickly refastened the oar and began rowing as fast as he could.

"I will row like an angry god, succumbing to death before I allow my arms to slow," he whispered though gritted teeth.

Shand pressed his lips together and inhaled deeply through his nose, then exhaled through his mouth and took a strong smooth stroke. He felt powerful and confident.

"They will catch you either way. You need to prepare."

Again, the voice was disembodied and floating behind his left ear, but Shand did not flinch this time. He stared straight and kept his focus aimed. If Shand remained still, he could almost see the voice in the corner of his eye—a charcoal grey, shadow-like presence. Shand tried turning his head to get a clear look. But no matter how quickly or slowly he turned, the presence would remain just outside of his sight.

"Why do you talk to me? Why have you moved from within my head? Hello!"

Shand felt that this added layer of emotion on his shoulders might break him. He felt the same confused panic creeping in as when he'd been deciding the fate of the rich woman. Trying to control it seemed futile. He could only channel the energy into the oars to keep it from boiling over, and Shand felt that just might save him.

Shand tore through the water like a whale, each stroke long and powerful. He dug deep with the oars, almost standing up to pull them through the water. The river flowed through the forest heavy and full. Its volume carried the boat downstream as if it were a feather. Shand felt like a soaring hawk catching headwinds as he bounced over the swells and powered downstream.

Glancing back and forth over each shoulder, he watched the upcoming banks for anything suspect. His mind saw images of the little demons perched in trees and crouched in bushes, patiently waiting to ambush him— capturing him to cook him alive over an open fire.

He expected to see another village or at least a boat out fishing, but the forest stayed dense with no signs of the little blonde devils.

He watched as the borders of the river gradually changed from heavy green grass to gnarled grey trees, extending their finger-like roots into to water, hanging their branches far and low over the river. The trees began to close in around him as the water narrowed into a fast-moving channel. He had to stop rowing and use the oars to steer away from rocks and keep the bow pointing downstream.

Shand was experienced with rapid water. In his village, if he wasn't fishing at sea with his uncle, then he was fishing alone on the Escaping River in his old tree-hollowed boat, and this river was a baby compared to it.

Just as Shand's shoulders began to burn, the river widened and slowed. He rested the oars and took a deep breath, listening to hear if the insects and birds were calling to him, warning him of the hunters—or alerting the hunters of him.

He could smell the sea and knew he had reached the mouth of the river. Shand stood to row for a while; the stretch felt good on his back and legs. With each stroke, the breeze grew stronger, and the heavy brown water melted into a deep grey.

He listened to the sounds of the woods fade into the sea breeze as the river opened wider and wider, then, finally, releasing him from the evil forest and birthing him into the sea.

He was free.

No more native demons. No more forest prison.

He felt like a found child.

The cool air tightened Shand's muscles, and he rowed faster to stay loose and warm.

He wanted to continue his journey southward, but his supplies were scarce, and the village of Stone Man was only two days north, so there was no real question. Stone Man was a friendly village in which he had rested on his way down the coast; it was named after the giant stone man extending from the side of a nearby cliff, kneeling down just inside the tree line, and looking over the beach and sea. The structure was best seen from the water and looked incredibly real from a distance.

As Shand rowed up the coast, an expanding relief lifted two stones from his weight. He felt like he had cheated death—a second life stolen from the gods.

His endurance was holding, so he rowed into the night just to make sure. There was a perfectly cool breeze, gently flowing under a heavy blanket of silence. He loved how quiet the sea could be; he called out to hear his voice quickly swallowed by its expanse, as if he was floating in the center of nowhere.

Shand watched the light move on the water as the moons crossed each other. He tossed his anchor and prepared a hook. The boat gently rocked with the swells as Shand thought of all that had taken place, reviewing every second since he had first stepped on that beach. He didn't realize it at first, but he was smiling.

He felt good and calm.

Shand must have dozed off, because his body jumped with a quick gasp of air, and he didn't know where he was for a second. He felt like something had happened.

He sat still, looking and listening. Everything seemed fine. No thunder, nothing. Shand remained perfectly quiet, not moving a muscle.

Then he heard it.

A faint sound, almost indistinguishable. But he knew what it was. Shand stood and squinted into the distance. He couldn't make anything out at first, but then he saw them.

Two small tree hollowed boats in a line, ten horses apart, two cannibals per boat.

Knowing he could never outrun them, Shand scurried around the boat searching for something. He was unsure of what that something was, but he felt he would know when he saw it. *"Let the little demons burn!"*

Shand paused and his eyes widened. "Yes!"

"Hurry! You don't have much time!"

Shand quickly pulled out Little Man and tightly wrapped the head in cloth, then doused the cloth with the alcohol from one of the jugs. He ripped his left sleeve off, tore it into pieces, then soaked the pieces in the alcohol, then stuffed the neck of each jug with the pieces, letting some hang out to be used as a wick.

He placed the axe and flint on the deck, then crouched to wait.

His timing had to be perfect.

As the boats drew closer, Shand could hear their paddles hitting the water and the soft splashes against their hulls.

His throat tightened.

He held fast, peering over the side as their blurry forms became clearer. He needed to wait until the last second before lighting Little Man and revealing his attack.

Just as the face of the native sitting at the bow of the first boat came into focus, Shand struck the flint hard. A beautiful spark hopped from the flint and ignited Little Man into a torch. He quickly lit the cloth hanging from the six jugs, and then stuck Little Man into the deck.

Passing the jugs from his left hand to his right, he barraged the first boat with fire bombs. The first two were direct hits, exploding the bow into a fireball. Shand could have sworn he saw the fireball transform into a flaming horse's skull screaming towards him as it glided just above the water.

"See! There is your proof! They are demons!"

His third throw landed perfectly, right under the rear native, engulfing the floor of the first boat in flames. The native jerked and kicked in the fire, rolling himself over the edge. Shand quickly grabbed the fourth jug just as the flaming boat was upon him. Impatient, he stupidly attempted to throw it directly at the native.

Luckily, the throw was short and clipped the tip of the bow, smashing the jug and throwing flaming alcohol all over the native. The native leapt from his seat, screaming. He danced around, trying to smack and pat the flames out like a panicked child.

Then suddenly he stopped, took a step back and positioned his feet.

45

"He's going to jump for it!"

The native's hair was on fire, along with the hair on the skins he wore. He looked like a true demon, strait from the fiery bowels of the underworld, and Shand was not sure he wasn't.

Just before the two boats made contact, the native took two steps and launched himself over the flames at Shand. Shand leapt up from his crouching position to meet him at full extension—shoulder to sternum, easily knocking the native back and off balance.

The native slipped and tumbled over the side but managed to grab the edge of the boat as he entered the water. Before Shand knew it, the native had his other hand on the side, pulling himself back in. Shand quickly pulled Little Man from the deck and began chopping back and forth at the native's hands. He managed to sever a couple of fingers before the native retreated to the water.

The second boat was closing fast, and Shand had no idea what to do next. Without thinking, he grabbed Little Man with both hands and swung him through the flames rising from the first boat, sinking the head into the inside of the its bow. His sleeves immediately caught fire, and he felt the heat singe his eyebrows. He set his feet, squatted, and with all his strength, jerked Little Man, pulling the front of the little boat up and onto his deck. Then one more tug to get it all the way on, accidentally putting the flaming bow just under the tent.

The hair on his furs caught fire along with parts of his own hair, and he was back-lit with a scene of flames and smoke from the burning tent. Now *he* was the flaming demon, and he felt like one too.

Shand ripped Little Man from the bow as the second boat made its approach. Then, with no plan and no thoughts, Shand hurled the flaming axe at the bow-seated native in the second boat. It hummed through the air like a spinning disc of fire, rapidly tumbling head over handle with almost no arc on its trajectory. A straight and fast line that ended in a miracle impalement of the native's forehead.

Shand froze, wide-eyed, as the native slowly slumped over, falling headfirst into the bottom of the boat. Shand was as shocked as the native had looked just before Little Man made impact. Shand quickly grabbed another jug, and this time made sure it landed *in* the boat. The rear native did not wait to be burned and hopped out before the jug made contact, giving the little boat a bit of extra momentum towards Shand.

Quickly, Shand leaned over the side, submerging his head and splashing out the flames on the skins. His hair and beard were burnt more than he had thought, singed and crunchy to blistered skin in some places. As the second boat coasted to a stop at Shand's stern, the three living natives came together, treading water and barking at each other.

Shand extinguished the remaining jugs, then stepped to the stern. He leaned over the edge, reaching into the second boat, then rolled the impaled native over and pulled Little Man from his head with one hard jerk. The three natives yelled and spit at Shand, but he paid no attention. They were helpless and they knew it. He removed an animal skin from the dead native's shoulders, then used it to smack out the smoldering tent. One of the natives had been able to hold onto a spear in the mayhem and tried to rise out of the water and throw it. But it was no use. His skins were too heavy, and the spear barely made it to the boat.

Shand smacked out the flames from the first boat, then splashed the flames out on the second boat before axing it and pulling it aboard too. He watched as the three yellow-haired bobbing devil heads turned calm and quiet, no yelling or barking, just watching Shand stone-faced, as he prepared to depart.

Shand's hands were burnt, along with the top of his head and brow. His eyebrows were gone and his beard was a smelted mess. The pain was just setting in, and he knew it would be a long couple of days to Stone Man.

As Shand rowed away, two natives swam to the dead native. They each grabbed an arm, then all three began the long swim to the beach, sharing the silence of defeat.

It was over.

Shand knew he would not see them again.

It did not take long for the preceding violence to leave Shand's body almost ill with fatigue. After rowing until his arms began to shake, Shand slid the two tree hollowed boats into the sea, then laid on the deck, his body completely drained and loose. He stared unfocused at one of the native's severed fingers resting on the deck as he drifted in and out of consciousness, his thoughts uncontrolled and free.

Through his haze, Shand saw a leaf float into view. It hopped and scraped along the deck, then came to rest against the finger. He watched the leaf twitch and move in the breeze. He felt his drool pool on the deck as he slipped further and further into a dead sleep.

That night, Shand dreamt like never before. His visions were vivid and real. The dreams were not of his family, boats, or savages. They were visions of sound, textures, and motion.

In the morning, Shand could hear his breath first. Then he saw the red and yellow swirls on the back of his eyelids; he knew it was light outside. But he could not move. He could not feel his limbs or his heartbeat. He could only feel the air entering and exiting his lungs.

Am I dying? He thought.

He tried to move, but could not. He tried to yell, but he was paralyzed.

As he lay still, listening and watching the swirls, he began to feel a tingle in his fingertips, then his toes. It took all he had, but he finally moved a finger. He focused on that finger to pull himself out of the darkness, slowly raising his limp body to a seated position. He felt like never before: like he hadn't completely returned, like he was in two places at once. He tried to recall his dreams, but they faded too quickly. Slowly, Shand was able to stand and stretch. Taking a deep breath, he wiped the crust from his eyes, then shuffled along the deck, scanning the shoreline and sea as his senses returned.

While Shand rowed that day, he daydreamed about the natives and the treasure. His dreams from the prior night slowly began to surface. All the strange images and feelings. Then, he saw the leaf. Partly with his mind and partly with his eyes. Identical to the one he had watched the night before, but enlarged. Enormous and beautiful.

As he rowed, the giant leaf drifted down from the sky and hovered just above the stern. Shand watched as the mirage grew vines from its points and attached to the boat. Feeling the vessel drag, he rowed harder, but the leaf was catching the breeze and slowed the boat to stop.

Suddenly, the leaf detached, then flew to the bow and disappeared.

A strange feeling filled his body. A vision grew in the center of Shand's mind like a flower opening its bloom. Shand felt like the sky was opening just for him, shining down a warmth he had never felt before. Everything became clearer and cleaner—a crisp edge on everything from his breath to the boards on the boat. A soft buzz warmed his brain. He had heard spiritual people and philosophers mention "inspiration," but he had never really known what it meant. Shand always thought it was about creating something unique or original. But now he saw that it was less about creating and more about uncovering, tearing back a layer to reveal something that had always been there.

CHAPTER III

The Family

Shand was eager to return home and tell Royce about his vision and all that had happened. But only a month or so had passed, and Shand did not want to give the impression of failure to his village, so he thought about staying in Stone Man for a while to work on his idea. He had made friends there with a fisherman named Lain.

Shand figured he could help Lain fish to earn his keep while he restocked supplies and worked on his big idea. He could figure out all the kinks, get everything working perfectly, and return to his village in glory. And if it ended in failure, no one would have to know.

Since he was able to swim, Shand had accompanied his uncle on almost every fishing trip and considered himself the second best fisherman in his village, only behind Royce himself. His family and the village assumed he would follow in his uncle's footsteps, but Shand did not like the idea of anyone other than himself selecting his role. He felt that he had experienced what he needed to from fishing, and was ready to move on.

When Shand was small, he and Royce had come across a traveler at sea. The traveler spoke a language that did not sound like words but drums, echoing deep from the man's stomach. His name was Tuma. He dressed in colorful flowing robes, and his skin was darker than Shand's people, almost the color of a dried Oak leaf. He had dark silk-like hair woven in a single braid that ran the length of his back. Shand vividly remembered the traveler's boat—long and thin, attached to an out-rigged boat-shaped piece of wood by two curved wooden poles. It was a brilliantly designed vessel—long and thin for speed—anchored to the out-rigged ski for stability. It was beautifully shaped and precisely constructed, painted in bright colors and intricate designs. The traveler had carried two paddles. The first had a short shaft attached to a wide blade that seemed to be woven of some type of bark. The second was longer than Tuma was tall, wielding a long, thin, solid wooden blade.

Royce was wary of the traveler, as he was with most things. But something about the man put Shand at ease: the way he communicated with his hands—expressive and joyful—and the rhythm of his voice—choppy, clear, and projected.

Shand and Royce had sat holding the sides of their boats together and watched the stranger's hands tell stories of his homeland. He made shapes with his hands that suggested huge structures, taller than anything Shand had seen. Shand hung on every gesture. His imagination raced faster than his memory, images his mind created from Tuma's descriptions constantly forgotten, replaced by bigger and better illustrations as the stories layered.

The thrill did not last as long for Royce. He began cutting eyes at Shand and signaling that it was time to go. But Shand pretended not to see Royce's signs, holding close attention to Tuma.

The stranger expressed the need for supplies, but Royce let him know he was not welcome to follow them back to the village. Shand protested, trying to explain to Royce that Tuma might have knowledge valuable to the village.

The traveler sat quietly, patiently listening to the two debate, holding out plants and spices as offerings. Finally, Royce had had enough. He pushed the boats away from each other, then banged on the side of their boat with his hand, yelling at the stranger and shooing him away.

Tuma's face seemed surprised and hurt—but it held a genuine smile for Shand as they rowed away. Like he *understood*. Shand watched what he thought could be his only connection to something *more* paddle his elaborate vessel onward, then disappear into the reflecting sunlight.

Shand never saw the man, nor anyone like him, again.

But the seed had been planted, and from that day forward, it stubbornly grew into a powerful desire for exploration, to which he was still a prisoner.

Shand wished his father, Tad, was still alive. He could have told him all about the savages and the treasure. They could have discussed the big idea, each becoming as excited as the other. His father would have been very proud.

Tad had drowned about a year ago after being overtaken by a squall on a solo fishing run. All Shand really remembered was standing on the bank, watching Alroy tow his father's empty boat back to dock. Shand had no memories of thoughts or emotions from that day, just the image of the empty boat, and the image of himself standing on the bank.

Shand and Tad had been very close. They were almost exact opposites, which, strangely, favored their relationship. Tad was always dreaming and philosophizing, trying to get others as excited about a recent epiphany as he was. He hated violence, loved to sing and dance, and was never reserved in showing love and affection for his family. His hair was golden with only a small hint of Shand and Royce's auburn tone, and he was taller and thinner than all of their relatives. He would embarrass Shand sometimes by saying strange things in public or acting like a boisterous child. It was like he was missing something, or had more of something. Shand could never really figure it out.

Shand, on the other hand, was introverted and loved being by himself to work or hunt. He had much more in common with Uncle Royce, Tad's brother. Shand had always been a bit scared of his uncle, especially his huge gnarled hands. He would stare at Royce's hands as they pulled and tied the nets, thinking they were almost inhuman. Royce never said much, but when he did, people listened. He was thick and sturdy. His beard nearly covered his entire face, and his eyes seemed to be in a constant squint. He was a solitary man, never married, no children. Shand respected his uncle, both for his strength and for his silence. Shand had learned at an early age that words had little value, and too often were even a detriment.

Sometimes, Shand thought he must really be Royce's son, and maybe there was some elaborate family deception. But, for some reason, he knew that was not true.

After his father's death, Shand's father's father, Alroy, a tall spicy-smelling old man with a sharp tongue, became the head of Shand's family, He was oddly strong, and he moved like a man in his prime. Shand and Alroy hardly knew each other, and Alroy expected more from Shand than Shand thought he should, so that arrangement had only lasted a couple of weeks before Shand moved himself behind Royce's cottage. Alroy was not horrible by any means. He was a good provider and teacher, and never tried to take over Shand's family, but he made it clear that his word would be the last. He remained living in his own home, but he stopped in often to make sure things were running the way he wanted.

Shand was the eldest, with insights and fundamental ideals that were not in agreement with Alroy's rigid, often short-sighted, black and white mentality. So Shand figured it would be best for everyone if he were on his own—not to mention, then Shand could finally build the boat of his dreams, the one in which he would explore unknown waters and undiscovered lands, the one he would ingeniously design for expedition, the one that would set him as free as a man could be.

Just before Shand's seventeenth birthday, he traded all he had of worth to Duncan, the local smith, in return for some old woodworking tools. Not having much of worth, he figured he could help Duncan at night to make up the difference, leaving his afternoons open to build, and his mornings free to help Royce fish and hopefully earn his keep in return.

One of Shand's most powerful memories was that night he stood in Duncan's doorway, just after Duncan had placed the tools in Shand's hands, and Shand was free from all other possessions.

He felt naked in the eyes of the all things. Almost scared. Like he was too free, loose and floating away.

For the first time he was truly on his own.

From that night forward, he worked nearly every night with the smith, learning more than he'd ever imagined. They forged hinges, pots, weapons— everything the village needed.

"My Grandfather is the smith who invented bronze," Duncan would tell Shand for the twentieth time, and then pause for the twentieth time to see Shand's reaction.

"Yes, I know, Duncan. He was a great man, like you," Shand always replied, never failing to bring a smile to both their faces.

Shand never knew if Duncan realized that he was old and that his memory played tricks on him. But Shand figured it didn't really matter either way.

Duncan was not just old, he was *very* old, so old that he didn't know how old he was, and the villagers were unsure because he had outlived all of his peers and had no family. His frame was thin, and he did not have an ounce of fat on his body. Every loose muscle was visible through his aged skin. He kept a short white beard and was nearly bald on top. His face was almost gaunt, and what teeth he had left were in bad shape. But he could work like a horse, outpacing anyone Shand knew, and his grip was even stronger than Royce's.

Duncan would crush walnut shells between his thumb and forefinger like they were pieces of dirt, smiling a devious smile at Shand while letting a few deranged chuckles escape from his belly. Shand could never determine exactly what Duncan was trying to say or show by the performance. He would always just smile back, and that seemed to satisfy the old man, or at least Duncan acted like it did.

Sometimes, Shand thought Duncan knew something he did not. Like Shand was merely a naïve child who had no idea what was really going on, and Duncan was humorously watching him fumble through life. But those thoughts were usually short-lived due to an enormous lack of evidence, so Shand went with the *crazy old man* theory more than not. In all, they enjoyed each other's company and got along well. Duncan found the son he had never had, and Shand got a crazy father again.

Shand had been in the process of building the roof that would cover the spine, planks, and supplies when he met Thief—a male adolescent shepherd, skinny and tall with a coarse black coat and brown markings around his snout and feet. Their eyes would occasionally meet through the brush, and Shand would hold his gaze, bending down and giving out sweet high-pitched calls and clicks. The sad animal would not look away like dogs usually do. He stared back, his pitiful eyes desperate for a master. But his body was a slave to caution, remaining statue-like or lying down to pant and whimper. Shand would try to entice the dog with scraps, placing them on a plate just over halfway between the two of them, then turn his back and pretend to work.

The dog never moved a muscle. (At least Shand never *saw* him move a muscle.) But by sunset each day, the plate would be miraculously licked clean.

Shand could never figure out how he was doing it. He tried entrapping the dog by faking asleep or hiding behind something, leaving the plate unguarded, but the dog was always too smart or too patient.

There was no doubt about his name: he was a thief, and the smoothest of one at that.

One afternoon, Shand decided to leave the plate empty. As usual, he ignored the dog and the plate. He laid on his back and began nailing the first of the hull planks to the boat's ribs and spine. It wasn't long before Shand heard the quiet steps of his new friend, closer than ever. Shand remained on his back, staring up and driving nails into the boards, not even glancing in Thief's direction. A large wet nose slowly appeared hovering above Shand's face. It thoroughly sniffed Shand's hair and eye patch, then gave two licks to his cheek. Shand slowly raised up to give a couple a strong strokes down Thief's head and back.

Before long, Shand and Thief were eating every meal together. Thief wanted to be with Shand and protect him, and in return, he wanted Shand's affection and instruction. Thief loved completing tasks and receiving praise. He would even grow irritable if not challenged enough and nip at Shand's hands. He preferred his back scratched just above his hips, and he often let Shand know about it, putting his backside in the way of whatever Shand was attempting to do. It was bothersome, but it made Shand smile and even chuckle sometimes, bringing him back to the world from his all-consuming boat-making. On cold nights, Shand would try and pull the sleeping dog up, away from his legs, to warm his body. But as soon as Shand dozed off again, Thief would return to curl up between his legs or stretch out along the side of his thigh.

Shand loved Thief. He thought Thief was the most loyal and smartest dog in history. He even thought Thief was beginning to understand what he said.

One rainy night, Shand abandoned his makeshift shelter and snuck into Royce's house to sleep. In the morning, Shand awoke to Royce tinkering around the kitchen. Royce said nothing about Shand sleeping in the house, only asking if Shand would like some breakfast. Shand folded the quilt he slept with but did not return it to the chest. He left it where he had slept next to the fireplace.

Shand did not sleep outside again.

Royce would come outside every so often to tour the construction site, silently strolling around with his fingers interlaced behind his back, whistling and kicking pebbles. He would bend over and run his fingers along a board or take a long look at something. Or he would wait for Shand to make eye contact, then raise an eyebrow. Shand knew what Royce was doing and tried to remain calm and quiet to win the little game. Sometimes, Shand could hold out long enough and Royce would finally speak, letting him know what was on his mind. Other times, Shand could not take it. "What is it?" he would snap, even before Royce reached the halfway point of his capacity for annoying behavior, which always made Shand feel a little guilty. He knew Royce loved him and only wanted the best for him. The least he could do was humor him.

When Royce did speak, his advice saved Shand from mistakes that would have cost him an unknown amount of correction time. Shand hated that he needed the help, but he knew it was essential in order to get on the water anytime soon. And Royce was not one to be inflated while he critiqued, so Shand didn't mind so much.

Royce had a habit of acting like he was Shand's older brother when he was bored, or if he just wanted to get a rise from Shand. He would intentionally irritate Shand or say something off-color to see how Shand would react. Shand embraced it since he had never had an older brother. He knew how he could poke at his younger siblings and thought it was a good thing.

By now, word had spread of *Shand and his big boat*. People began stopping by to give their critiques, compliments, or both. Mostly, they had ideas of how something Shand had already done could have been done better. He took offense at first, but soon realized that mostly everyone was just being nosey, and they didn't really know anything about anything.

Shand loved when his siblings came by. They seemed in awe of Shand and wanted nothing but the best for him. Shand would sneak them pieces of advice on how to survive their mother and grandfather in an attempt to deepen his relationship with them and help their futures at the same time. His mother, Ana, would make sure he was feeling okay, eating well, and had everything he needed. She had always been the head of the family, and on the surface seemed stern to the point of unloving. But underneath she had a soft heart. She tried to show her care through sacrifice, but too often her offerings were overlooked by selfish eyes.

Ana's hips and legs were heavy, but her largeness was disguised by her grace. Her waist was narrow, and she moved with a powerful ease that made Shand think she could break him over her knee. Her hair and complexion were the color of young wheat. The skin on her face was extraordinarily smooth, thick and tight across her large cheekbones and wide forehead. She wore her hair in a bun, pulled tight on top, which rounded off her rigid look.

Shand had thought about his parents as colors, one yellow, the other blue, combining to create green. A new and unique color with no remnants of the former. But as he aged, he realized the colors did not completely mix, leaving stubborn slivers of blue and yellow churning inside him to be revealed when he least expected it.

When the weak-hearted stopped by Shand's construction site, they usually just made comments insinuating Shand thought himself to be superior, and of course point out when something didn't look right. He would hear things like: "He must think he's too good for us," and, "What is he trying to prove?" The amount of people hoping for his failure exceeded those who wanted him to succeed by a large and unexpected margin. But Shand was not bothered. In a strange way, it encouraged his spirit. For some reason, the more he heard the people's negativity, the more he knew he would be successful.

After months of labor, mistakes, and long nights, the boat was finally ready to be launched. It took Shand, Royce, Ana, and Duncan to balance the boat while Royce's mule pulled the vessel over the roller logs. Shand's golden-haired fourteen-year-old sister, Banan, and his orange-haired twelve-year-old sister, Catrin, were in charge of moving the logs from the back to the front of the spine as they slowly rolled to the dock. Baird, also known as "Little Shand," was too young to really help, besides keeping his eye on the youngest of the litter, Filib, a mischievous fat toddler who wore a constant slobbery smile.

Filib was everyone's favorite. Shand's sisters would fight over who slept with Filib at night, and Baird was always trying to see what he could get Filib to do—eat bugs, kick his sisters, and even slightly dangerous things for which Catrin and Banan would punish Baird. Sometimes, Baird would receive dirt in his mouth or spit in his face from the girls for even mentioning something that could hurt their sweet Filib.

When they released the boat, it pushed into the sea like a stone, almost taking on water, then rose to bob back and forth before coming to a beautiful rest.

Shand smiled.

His body tingled with warmth that reminded him of being a child and experiencing wonder for something new. It was a feeling like no other. He could only stand and stare as Royce jumped aboard to search for leaks. He watched in a daze as his siblings followed, but unlike Royce, they began running and jumping all over his boat, actions that ripped Shand from his daze into a mild frenzy.

"Quit running around!" Shand yelled. "Get off there! Only Royce and I!"

His brothers and sisters listened when Shand spoke, especially when he yelled. Ana did not have to try very hard to get her clan under control. They did not like seeing Shand angry. Shand told them that he and Royce needed to work now, but they would soon have everything ready, and they could come back in a few days for a ride.

"I'll sneak back and ride your boat after you go to bed," Duncan joked.

Shand did not smile, but everyone else did.

From that day on, Shand spent every day and night on his boat, adding finishing touches, constructing the tent canopy, packing, then forgetting something, then reorganizing and repacking. Royce joined him in the afternoons to help, but mainly to drink wine and speculate. Shand loved being on his boat. He could sit for hours just looking at it, thinking it was the most balanced and perfect thing in the world. It was the first time Shand had created something that took so much from him. He felt it was almost an extension of himself.

One afternoon, Shand and Royce were relaxing on the deck after a long day of preparing when a crowd of villagers shuffled by. As they strolled around, they would slow, then huddle in groups, whispering and pointing, then slightly disperse, only to weed around, forming new groups to whisper and point. It was almost like the crowd was its own entity, changing and developing, growing stronger to better suit its purpose of validating like-minded opinions.

While Shand studied the villagers, he began to feel disconnected. For the first time, he did not see them as individuals, but as one. That made him feel guilty.

Shand wondered if he did perceive himself as superior.

He had always thought his desire came from a place of curiosity and a passion for adventure, not ambition or vanity.

Shand was confused. But he knew one thing; he did not feel connected to them the way they felt connected to each other.

Shand visited his family the night before his big departure to say goodbye and eat what he thought could be his last home-cooked meal. His mother and sisters did not want to say goodbye. They were frightened for Shand and at the possibility they would never see him again.

"Why do you have to go for so long?" Ana pleaded.

Catrin tried to reason with Shand. "Why can't you just go on short trips, a little farther each time?"

Banan was not so cordial. She and Shand were the most alike in the family, neither giving value to insincere politeness for the purpose of unity, or to social formality in any form.

"I thought you were smarter than this!" she exclaimed.

"This is a stupid decision, and you need to think about it… Selfish! Selfish!" she yelled as she stormed off, of course in hopes that Shand would come after her and she could keep him on her hook.

But Shand knew her game.

"You know I'm leaving either way," he called. "You better come give me a hug while you can."

Banan waited as long as she could, then, as usual, came running from the back of the house to jump into Shand's arms, squeezing his neck and gritting her teeth.

Baird, on the other hand, was more than excited, pulling on Shand's clothes and yelling, "Bring me back something great! A skull of a beast you killed! Or a special weapon!"

"Hopefully," Shand replied, with wide eyes and an echoing voice, "I'll bring you something you can't even imagine."

Baird jumped and danced around, grabbing at his sisters and brother. They resisted at first, but soon gave in, transforming the evening's mood from somber to joyful. They all danced around, laughing and listening to Baird sing about Shand exploring the world and fighting sea monsters.

It was a good night.

After the last and longest hug with Ana, Shand and Thief headed back to the boat for the night. Thief trotted a little closer to Shand than usual, looking up at Shand often with concerned eyes. He knew Shand was leaving and was unsure if he was coming back.

In the morning, Shand awoke before sunrise to Thief's nails anxiously pacing the dock. Shand dragged himself out of the boat and onto the dock to sit and hang his feet off the side. He called Thief with his usual two-note whistle, but Thief did not want to surrender, turning in circles and whining. Shand managed to reach out and start a good scratch on Thief's rear that mildly settled the little beast.

As the sky slowly came to light, Thief became strangely calm. He stared off the dock, deep into the horizon, not looking back at Shand as usual, but gazing steadily, mouth open, panting deep and slow.

"Make your first trip shorter than you're thinking," Royce's voice boomed from the quiet. Shand jumped and turned around to see his uncle squinting in the morning sun, smiling an unusually large smile. He was strapped with rope and a couple of bags that Shand was sure were precautionary supplies for his voyage.

It had never been discussed, but Shand knew Royce would be there to see him off.

It was just understood.

Looking at Royce's smiling face in the morning light, Shand had a brief wash of clarity. He realized that everyone and everything instinctually knew its place. His family, himself, Thief, the trees, the birds, everything. He did not know how often these truths were submitted to, or if they were seen at all. But he felt that, in the deepest and most serious circumstances, submission became a nonnegotiable law of nature.

The clarity quickly passed, never to be fully seen again, but Shand knew he could hold onto its truth by remembering the feeling it had brought. Shand always tried to recall that feeling when being confused about someone's intentions or the context of sarcastic dialogue.

After getting the boat settled and warning Shand of everything he could think of, Royce gave Shand an unprecedented hug. Shand did not want to tell Royce that he had no intentions of returning anytime soon, maybe ever.

Shand gave Thief a long hug and a few hard pets, then Royce tossed the lines in the boat and pushed it away from the dock. Thief did not try and board. He sat at Royce's feet, softly whimpering. As Shand rowed away, Royce did not tinker around the dock. He stood still while they watched each other shrink into the distance, both knowing this could be Shand's first and last adventure.

CHAPTER IV

The Bear

Shand was nearing his physical and mental limits when he saw the flickering torches lining the dock at Stone Man. His stroke had deteriorated to less than half its usual length, and it felt better on his neck muscles to hang his head. His mouth and nose were so dry that it hurt to take a deep breath. His mind was too weary to produce emotions, or even to concentrate on a specific thought.

One more stroke was all he knew.

"Just one more stroke," the voice whispered calmly every time Shand thought he might be on his last row.

He could not feel his arms strain, or his back pull the oars through the water. His body was numb.

It had taken Shand two full days to return to Lain's village. Having no water, he pushed himself too hard to get there before he thought his body might shut down, which resulted in a thirst Shand had never experienced—dry and deep, like a hunger that came from his bones, smothering the pain from his burns like they weren't even there. He could have stopped and tried to find water, but given what had happened the last stop, he decided to risk the thirst.

It began to sprinkle as Shand made his last few strokes to the dock. He pulled the oars in, then raised his head back and opened his mouth.

Water had never tasted so good.

Shand's weak legs shook as he stood and wobbled back and forth, trying to get the rope over the piling. As he stumbled to the deck to lie down, the clouds opened and emptied a sheet of continuous rain onto the sea.

Shand laid on his back, letting the cool rain fill his mouth. He closed his eyes and listened to the sound of a million raindrops splashing into the sea. Like a constant growing echo, the sound deepened as Shand's arms and legs relaxed to dead weight and his fingers and toes went numb. He began to hear a million smaller raindrops falling among the first million, some landing in concert, others just off rhythm. His neck and head loosened, allowing the warm tingle rising from his spine to enter his head and open his ears even farther, to hear yet another million tiny drops falling in between the smaller drops, pushing the harmony fuller and heavier, until his ears, his mind, and the sea were saturated with a beautiful hum that was so enveloping it became his dreams. No images, no motions or textures. Just the deep hum wrapping him in a blanket of sound.

He slept like he did as a child, deep and free.

Shand awoke calmly to the morning sun. He felt good and rested. A pool of water had collected on the deck where the tent used to be. As Shand learned over to take a drink, he caught his reflection in the puddle. He almost did not recognize himself. He looked like he had been pulled from his grave. His bad eye was uglier than he remembered, looking more like a dead fish's eye than his scary demon eye. His skin was sunburnt and fire-burnt along his brow and forehead in a painful bloody crust. His eye sockets were sunken and weak, and he could see bones in his face that he had never seen before. His mouth seemed larger and less human. He stared at himself like he was looking through a hole in the deck that connected two worlds, and some strange ravaged animal was looking back at him.

Shand's hypnosis was broken by the sound of voices on the bank. He looked up to see the village's fisherman making their way to the dock for the morning run. Shand recognized the quick pace and wide gait of his friend right away. Lain was short and stocky. He did everything quickly, from talking to walking, which could wear on Shand's nerves a bit; but Lain got a lot done and Shand respected that.

Lain did not recognize him and took a step back when Shand approached, holding his hand out to declare his space. Shand thought it would be funny to tease his friend and pretend he was some sort of demon, there to bring Lain back to the underworld with him.

"I have come to take you home, my boy," Shand said in the deepest voice he could manage, crooking his legs and staggering toward Lain.

The joke was not thought out well and not received well either. Lain was not scared, nor did he have time for whatever this beggar was trying to scheme. Lain smacked Shand on the side of his head, driving him to his knees.

"What are you thinking?" Lain yelled, taking a step back and positioning himself for a kick.

"Wait! Wait! It's I! Shand! Shand!"

Lain paused, and Shand thought he just might kick him anyway.

"You fool! What's wrong with you? You're lucky I didn't crack your skull."

Half giggling, Shand apologized. "Sorry, sorry, my friend. I never knew you were so hostile to the weak."

"Not funny," Lain replied, pulling Shand to his feet. "You look worse than awful, my friend. What happened to you?"

Shand just smiled.

"Never mind. Let's get you inside." Lain said.

Shand bathed and trimmed his half-burnt beard into what resembled a tight high-class beard, which he hated. Lain's wife, Beitris, warmed some stew while Lain found clothes for Shand.

Shand was more than happy to sit at a table with civilized people and enjoy a warm meal and conversation. He felt at home, and he hadn't realized it until then, but he had a lot to express. He began to tell Lain and Beitris about his adventure, but after just a few sentences, Lain stopped him and said, "I need to make us a couple of drinks and get comfortable for this."

Lain skipped the morning fishing and sat in awe, listening to the incredible story while Shand cut and threaded a new eye patch. He made a habit of covering his eye out of courtesy in choice company, but he had packed his patch away the first day into his expedition, and now it was probably being worn as an accessory by one of the little native girls. It had been made for him by Banan for his thirteenth birthday. She had stitched a star in the center, which Shand was having a terrible time trying to recreate.

"Don't worry about the star!" Beitris insisted. "Give it to me. I will do it! Just tell me more about these savages."

Shand worried that he might not do their wickedness justice, so he embellished their ghostly black eyes and chattering speech. Little blonde monsters might not have the same effect verbally as they did in person. Shand climaxed the story with the amazing axe throw, leaving Lain's face with an expression of disbelief. But Shand didn't care; he expected it. What could be better than experiencing something that was unbelievable, but absolutely true?

Shand left out the part about his vision, of course. He wanted to make sure he had something viable before running his mouth, and there was no need to mention *the voice* either. No good could come from releasing such information.

Beitris tossed the patch to Shand. "I could have done better, but you had already messed it up," she said, loud enough to make sure both Lain and Shand heard.

The morning ended in laughter, with Shand trying on the pitiful eye patch and stumbling around like he was a drunken vagabond.

"You know you can stay here as long as you need," Lain reassured him.

"Thank you, my friend, but I would not feel right infringing on your and Beitris's privacy. My boat is plenty for me," he replied, pulling Lain in with a firm forearm shake. "But I do have one thing to ask of you."

"Anything," said Lain.

"Let me fish with you. I am a great fisherman, and I could help you catch more fish than any other. All I ask is that I keep half the fish we catch over the amount of your regular haul."

"Well, well," Lain snickered. "You have your own boat, and I'm sure a great fisherman like yourself has all the necessary supplies. What do you need with me?"

Shand smiled. "I don't need you. It's a favor to you. I would never want to put my friend out of work."

Lain gave a chuckle and Shand smiled, neither knowing how serious the other was.

Shand spent the next few weeks helping Lain fish. He showed Lain a few dragnet techniques and Lain showed Shand the thinnest, strongest line he had ever seen.

"How did you make this?" Shand questioned.

"I didn't," replied Lain. "A seamstress known as Bear gave it to me."

"Bear? Is she mean like a bear, or just the size of one?"

"Bear is someone you just have to see for yourself. You should pay her a visit. Maybe pretend you need some line or netting."

Shand decided he would definitely pay her a visit. But he didn't have to pretend to need anything. A great seamstress was a necessity for his invention.

Shand lived up to his word. Once he and Lain became familiar with one another's working habits, they made a great team, easily having the best catch in the village every day.

Shand had plenty to barter with, and even had to travel to a few river communities inland to trade with the surplus. He gave a portion of his catch to the local smith in return for copper, tin and the use of his equipment at night. Shand felt that working with Duncan had been the most valuable thing he had ever done. That knowledge could never be taken like gold, silver, or even power.

Shand forged two bronze sleeves. The first sleeve was anchored on a hole Shand had cut into the deck between the oars and the bow. He anchored the second sleeve to the spine directly below the first sleeve.

It took longer than Shand had thought to find a tree trunk for his deck post. He wanted a hard wood as close in shape to the final product as possible to minimize labor, but he had no luck finding one that wasn't too large or too erratically shaped. Finally, he settled for a young pine. It was light, straight, and almost the exact diameter he needed.

Shand debarked and cut the trunk to length on site. The less commotion he made around the village the better. The last thing he needed was more nosy villagers prying into his business. He worked into the night, shaving the bottom portion of the trunk so it could slide in and out of the sleeves with just the right fit.

He waited until it was late and the village was quiet to make his way back. He laid the thinner end of the post just over the center of a long, thin hide strap, and then tied a knot in the center of the strap, gripping the post. He then pulled the two ends of the strap over each shoulder and dragged the post like a mule. Gripping the straps at his chest, he leaned into each stride with a small lunge before each step.

Shand underestimated the difficulty of the move. He handled it fine at first; it even felt lighter than expected. But by the time he navigated the log through the woods and around the village, so no one would see him, he was more than exhausted.

He dropped the end of the post on the dock next to his boat, releasing his hands from the painful strangle of the strap. His lower back loosened and a sharp pain traveled the length of his spine as he stood up straight. A deep groan left his body uncontrollably as he stretched and cracked his limbs.

After Shand filled his belly with water and mildly regained his strength, he rested the thick end of the post on the edge of the deck sleeve, then lifted the other end over his head. The end of the pole stayed stationary against the inside edge of the deck sleeve opening as he walked towards the sleeve, raising the post hand under hand. When the post was almost vertical, he rotated himself around, then kicked the end of the post off the sleeve's edge, sending the post sliding through the deck sleeve and into the spine sleeve perfectly. Tight, but not too tight, easily removed to hide the operation by day.

"I'm brilliant!" he announced to the sea. "And I am coming!"

"Slow down. You've done nothing yet."

Shand paused, but he was not startled this time. He was too happy about his progress. "Where have you been?" Shand replied confidently. "I haven't heard from you in a while. I was beginning to think I was free from you."

"You haven't needed me in a while."

"I have never needed you."

"You need me more than you know, and I need to protect what's mine."

"What does that mean? There is no sense in speaking in riddles. I am in control and will never acknowledge you again if I see fit."

"You are a thief!" boomed the voice, clearer and more human than ever before.

"Leave me alone! I have stolen nothing, and I am growing tired of you."

"Can't you feel it? Can't you see you don't fit? I know you sense it. You are a liar!"

"I am done with this game. You do not even exist—a figment of my imagination brought on by fatigue and isolation. I will ignore you into extinction."

Shand began vigorously removing the post, feeling like keeping busy would help keep the voice away. Maybe it worked, or maybe it was the voice's choice, but he heard nothing else that night.

After removing the deck post and floating it under the dock to keep it out of sight, Shand tried keeping busy by cleaning and going over plans in his head. He came to the conclusion that he needed to get the fabric figured out as soon as possible.

Not much sleep came to Shand that night. He kept expecting *the voice* to yell out, or whisper something sinister in his ear. His stomach felt hollow, and his head was filled with a pressure he could hear. Although he felt very tired, his body was painfully awake. He had never felt so uneasy and irritated from within, like something deep inside had come loose.

The sunrise brought on better feelings. His stomach was settled, and his head felt almost normal. He was eager to start a new day, and even more eager to meet the "Bear" lady.

Lain told Shand to follow the southern path until he reached the large pines; the woman's home would be just over the second hill. Lain wore a strange smile, which he seemed to be trying to hide; that made Shand's imagination run.

Is he setting me up for a joke? He thought. Is the woman deformed and wild or something?

During his walk, images of the woman and her lair grew and compounded uncontrollably in Shand's mind, stretching from a female bear wearing clothes and living in a tree trunk to a skinny old lady with a bear's jaw waiting to eat him.

Shand walked the entire morning before coming to the pine forest. He couldn't believe she lived so deep in the woods alone.

Or *did* she live alone?

He had never thought to ask, nor had anyone mentioned it. He had just assumed a bear would live by itself.

That could be the joke. Something about her cubs or husband.

As Shand topped the first hill, he caught a whiff of smoke. It was the scent of a pine fire, possibly Shand's favorite smell. Anytime he smelled that scent, he was instantly transported into memories. Memories of small cooking fires on overnight hunting trips with Royce and his father. Memories of walking back home, cold, wet, and hungry from a day out fishing or hunting, then smelling the smoke from the fire burning inside his family's cottage, and imagining what everyone was doing inside all warm and cozy

As Shand ascended the second hill, he saw the haze from the smoke rising into the canopy. His insides grew anxious at what he was about to see. Shand lay down at the top of the hill and slowly peeked over the ridge.

What he saw was beautiful: a large glade dotted with giant pine trees with the largest trunks he had ever seen, stretching high into the forest before sprouting branches. There was almost no undergrowth, just a thick blanket of pine needles layering the forest floor. A circular stone dwelling with a beveled thatched roof rested perfectly next to a small stream. If he was a hermit, Shand thought, this is where he would live.

Shand's anxiousness quickly grew into excitement to meet the resident, or residents. No matter if they were deformed or crazy. At the least they had to be interesting.

"Hello...hello!" Shand politely called out before reaching the dwelling. He softly tapped on her door, then waited. There was no answer, so he tapped a little harder.

Still no answer.

Just as Shand was putting his hand on the handle, the door swung open. Shand jumped back, frozen, his eyes locked on a vision of the most beautiful young woman he had ever seen.

She was tall and slender, with golden hair and a warm complexion. She wore a heavy pair of leather boots and a mid-calf cream dress under a snug-fitting brown leather vest with thick laces running up the front. The clothes were unlike anything he had seen. He was used to women wearing skins and loose-fitting leathers and dresses.

Her lips were light pink along with the tip of her nose and cheeks. She had large clear eyes with deep blue-grey irises. She was strong in the hips and shoulders, her joints thin and delicate.

Shand could not make words. He could only wait for her response to his presence. But she just stared. No smile, no frown.

She must be scared to death of me, he thought.

Shand managed to force out the only word he could find.

"Fabric," he whispered. "Fabric."

The young woman's body language instantly changed. She put her hand on her hip and relaxed her stance, then titled her head and smiled a smile that Shand knew he would never forget.

She stepped back and opened the door wider. "Come in."

Shand had not completely recovered from the shock of her beauty, and he felt dizzy as he stepped through the doorway. She shut the door behind them, and he was quickly enveloped with the scent of her space. His knees weakened, causing him to misstep and stumble a bit. She acted like she didn't notice the trip, but he could see her half-hidden smile. His senses were heightened like when he had battled the native, but different this time—less sharp and painful, more like a warm blooming. He could smell everything, almost individually—the hovering remnants of a heavily-spiced potato stew, the wildflower arrangements in thin colorfully-painted ceramic vases, the smoldering fire in need of another log…and most of all, her scent entwined with all things in her home.

Shand was quickly snapped out of his trance as she grabbed his wrist and excitedly pulled him through her home, explaining how she had created a tool that allowed her to weave high-quality fabrics, ten or even twenty times faster than before, and how she could make large sections of fabric without help.

Shand had never met anyone like her. She moved freely and spoke with a unique confidence. She maintained deep eye contact when talking directly to Shand, which intimidated him at first, but he could feel her warmth and honesty and quickly became comfortable with her.

Shand was interested in her tool and tried to pay close attention as she passed a piece of wood attached to a single thread through separated vertical pieces of thread, then slid a stick down between the vertical threads and did something with her foot. But he was too distracted by her to concentrate on what she was doing.

Standing behind her as she explained, he could watch her uninterrupted—the way she spoke and the grace of her movements as she worked. It was like he had inhaled a warm sweet mist that lingered in every crevice of his body. He was calm, content, and, for the first time, there was no debate or the usual introspection.

He wanted her to be his, and that would not change.

Shand tried to play it cool and keep the dialogue about business. That way, he could keep the conversation flowing and would not stumble over words or say something strange, coming off as desperate or powerless to her beauty. He knew this type of woman would never be attracted to a meek man—a man to be controlled, abused at will, like a tool whose only purpose was to improve the woman's life.

This woman would only give herself to an equal, someone worthy of respect, someone to share her life with. He wanted to have her more than anything before, more than his boat, more than even his freedom to explore. It was almost painful. He wanted to love her, and he wanted her to love him in return. Shand felt like his life had been turned upside down, as if an omnipotent force had stampeded out of nowhere and run him over.

Shand tried to prolong his visit as long as he could, making up questions he already knew the answers to, or pretending he was unsure of exactly what he needed. When she asked what the giant cloth was for, he said it was for a tool that he had invented; like hers, it could improve how things were done. But he had to keep it a secret.

She did not ask why, only smiled.

He felt like he had won the first battle—her interest.

Shand was careful not to stay to the point of awkwardness. He knew he would see her again, so he offered a swift and careless goodbye in hopes of giving her an impression of strength.

Shand felt like his feet were floating just above the ground on the walk back home. He could not push Bear's image out if his head. A replay of the evening continuously rolled in his mind. She was all he could think about, and all he wanted to think about.

Bear told Shand it would take a long time to weave the tight and very thin sheet of fabric he needed, and his project would have to be put aside often to complete smaller jobs. Shand did not mind; it just meant he would have a connection to her for longer.

"You know she will never love you."

"You're back!" Shand declared. "The little powerless demon voice. I was wondering where you went."

"You are the demon! And an imposter! I can't believe you really think she will love you and you can have a real life. You must be more lost than I thought."

"Your madness and lies grew tired long ago. You are wasting your time."

"Time is all I have. You have stolen all else from me—my body, my family, my memories, my dog and now maybe my wife. My patience has run out. I will invade you like you did me, and we will finally meet in battle."

"Wow! I'm frightened! It only took me supposedly stealing absolutely everything you had before you decided to battle? It sounds like you are weaker than I thought."

"You cannot have a real life. You are not human. You are a lost demon that possessed my body when I was weak. You cannot win. You are just a sad and lonely demon that has lost its way. You do not belong here, and I know you feel it. This is an endeavor you cannot achieve. You must look deep inside, allow me to return, let me in when you feel me push, and it will make us both whole again. You are only hurting yourself and prolonging the inevitable."

"Your manipulation is laughable. If I am a demon, then why have you not battled me before now?"

"I was too weak, and like you before, stuck, floating back and forth between two worlds. But soon I will have all my strength and will claim what is mine."

"Come and get it."

Shand was visibly shaken. His legs and hands had to keep busy or they would tremble. He tried to remain calm, but the voice had never sounded so strong before. He needed to find a healer as soon as possible.

The next morning, Shand arrived at the dock at sunrise as usual. Lain had gotten there early and already had the boat prepared. Before Shand reached the boat, Lain shouted with a bright face and a wicked smile, "How'd you like Bear?"

Shand knew it was coming, but he had to play calm. What kind of fool falls in love with a woman after only the first meeting?

"She was very pretty. As I'm sure you know," Shand responded.

"And smart, too, right?" Lain smirked.

"Yes, and I presume you think I'm in love with her now."

"Not at all, my friend. I *know* you are in love with her."

Shand laughed and pretended to arrange the nets in a better position. But Lain did not move. He stood still staring at Shand's face with that signature, irritating smile—unique to Lain.

Don't smile, Shand thought. Look him square in the face, and don't smile.

Shand looked up from the nets directly at Lain. But as soon as their eyes met, Shand felt the blush instantly grow from his guts, rushing up his chest and into his face, burning his cheeks and warming his ears.

"Ha! Ha! Ha! Ha!" Lain bellowed. "I knew it. Your face looks like a five year old's!"

"Oh! Be quiet," Shand groaned. "She was pretty, yes, and smart, but I am no weak-hearted fool."

"Don't feel bad, my friend. Everyone I know has been in love with the beautiful Bear at one time or another. No man who's met her has not tried to have her. You are no different, so don't even try and pretend to be too strong. It's not a matter of strength, anyway. It's a matter of her magic, and now, my young friend, it's a matter of…if you can get her… Am I right?"

Lain chuckled, patting Shand on the back. "No need to respond. Just know I am here for you."

Shand felt silly, but also strangely comforted by Lain's words.

"Tell me about the other men," Shand asked.

As they fished, Lain told Shand of the numerous men, including himself, who had competed for Bear's affections. He told Shand that some in the village even thought she must not be interested in men, or that she might not even be all human.

"Some believe she's involved in dark magic and has no need for human desires—but of course the worst rumors are perpetrated by the most heartbroken."

"That is ridiculous!" Shand announced. "She is the kindest, most honest creature I have ever met!"

"I know, I know," Lain snickered, continuing in a teasing high-pitched voice. "But some say the worst demons come in the best disguises."

"Why is she called Bear?" Shand questioned.

"Well, there are a few stories floating out there. She always told me that she had no idea why people called her Bear… The most popular story is that she ripped out a man's throat with her teeth after he persisted with unwanted advances… Some said a female bear that had killed her parents raised her… Others say she becomes a bear at night with her magic."

Shand wrinkled his forehead and stared into the distance. They fished in silence for the remainder of the day, Shand's mind compulsively sifting through scenarios about Bear's life, Lain giving his friend space to wonder.

Shand concluded that he needed to get his priorities straight and see a healer before he even thought about anything else. He lied about the voice and told Lain there was a strange pain in his stomach that would not go away. Lain told Shand to visit the village elder, whose name was Boshil.

"He has helped me before," Lain said, "and Beitris, too, when she was pregnant. Just don't see Conn. He is a senile fool who will spit on you and rub you with sticks."

Shand was unsure how he was going to tell the healer about his situation. He thought about making up a story about how a relative was hearing a voice. But he was afraid Boshil might not believe him and label him possessed.

He had only seen one man whom people called possessed. Shand had been no more than seven years old. He had purposefully forgotten most of the experience, but vividly remembered the burning and insect bites inflicted upon the man at the hands of the so-called healers—how the focus of the treatment quickly changed from helping the man to making sure the demon inside him did not survive, resulting in the man's death and merely the presumed death of the demon, guaranteed only by the word of the healer.

Shand felt uneasy as he approached Boshil's home. Something did not sit right about the scene. He did not know why, but he stopped. He stared at the cracked mortar between the carelessly placed stones. He looked at Boshil's poorly constructed door and its uneven gaps. It could have been made so much better. His home seemed dirty and unkempt in general.

What kind of man could heal but not clean or build? Maybe that was why he healed, because he could do nothing else, and that was why he had chosen a craft in which an evidence of worth was not integral.

Shand thought he would be better off facing the demon alone.

He spent the next few days fishing, acquiring the ropes of varying diameter he thought he needed, and carving the two cross-poles that would run across the deck post. He wanted to return to Bear's home as soon as he could without seeming desperate, and he figured five days would be appropriate—a reasonable time to check on the sheet's progress.

Shand wanted to bring her a gift, but not an obvious or careless gift. He wanted to give her something perfect, something she needed without knowing it. He could act like it wasn't even a gift. Just something he'd run across that he thought she could use. He used the next couple of days to try and figure out what that something was. He knew it was out there; he just couldn't quite call it out.

Finally, he asked Beitris what she thought about a gift for Bear, and pleaded with her not to mention it to Lain. He did not need the extra ribbing, he explained. She agreed, and told him that every woman loves jewelry, anything shiny and pretty that makes her feel shiny and pretty.

"Anything else?" Shand asked. That was far too unoriginal for Bear. It had to be special.

"Flowers, maybe?" Beitris offered. "We all love flowers."

Shand thanked her for her help and told her he would try and find a unique bracelet or necklace. He was disappointed, but he figured giving Bear nothing at all was far better than something average.

On the morning of the fifth day, Shand trotted down the path to Bear's home with a grin on his face he could not wipe off. He could not wait to be in her home again, in her presence. He attempted to knock on her door with a friendly medium knock, not too heavy and overbearing, not too light and unsure.

The door almost immediately opened, like she had been waiting just behind it. Her face was bright and smiling, even more beautiful than before. She stepped aside like before to let Shand enter. Neither of them spoke, but there was an energy Shand could feel that had not been there before. She held out her hand to show Shand a small red pouch.

"I made this for you," she said with a smile.

Shand was taken aback, his voice about to tremble. "You made something for me?"

"Well, you needed it, and it was no big problem."

Shand opened the pouch to find the most perfect and beautiful eye patch he had ever seen. It was made from hardened hide, dyed deep brown, convex and shaped to fit snugly under his brow and along his cheekbone. She had recreated Banan's star with bone-colored thread stitched to perfection, then bordered the patch with the same stitching. The hide band was attached by the border stitches on the back of the patch and dyed to match.

Shand did not know how to respond. He was speechless. His heart filled, and he felt like it was going to overflow and make his eyes water.

"Thank you," he said. "I love it."

The words came out clear and strong, because they were the absolute truth. Bear smiled and gave him a side hug. It was the most physical contact they'd had, and Shand wondered if she felt the same incredible warmth he did. He was surprised that he felt almost guiltless for not having a present for her; any guilt was too far buried under his disbelief and excitement that she had given him one.

"Come see your sheet!" Bear grabbed Shand's hand and trotted him to her weaving room.

He loved everything about her—the way she lightly scooted through the house, the feel of her hand in his, the way she could experience joy like a child.

He felt like he was home.

Bear proudly showed Shand his sheet in progress. She put a corner in his hand and rubbed her fingers over his, showing him the thickness and quality of the sheet. "It's what you are looking for, right?"

"Yes, yes, it's perfect."

Bear smiled up at Shand, keeping eye contact a little longer even than normal.

For the rest of the day, the two talked, laughed, and pretended to work, standing just close enough to be in each other's space. For lunch, they sat on the same side of the table, pretending to accidentally touch legs on occasion.

Shand was sure she felt the connection between them. He had never felt a love for someone like that before. Unlike the secure deep-rooted love for his family and friends, it was more intense and constant. He did not want to leave, and he could tell she did not want him to leave either. He knew she would not invite him to stay, and asking to stay was not an honorable option.

As dusk fell, all Shand could think about was kissing her goodnight. There would be no careless goodbye this time. He felt like he needed evidence of his assessment.

Shand told Bear it was getting late and that he had better head back before he lost the light. He helped her clear the table, then slowly headed for the door, giving her plenty of time to see him out. He opened the door and took a half step out, then fully turned to face her. His stomach tightened, and he could feel his heartbeat. But to his surprise, the next move was made for him, as Bear grabbed both his hands, leaned up and gave him a kiss on the cheek.

"When are you coming back?" she said.

Shand was taken aback, and had trouble making clear thoughts. "Uh, um, in a few days, maybe?"

His body was stiff and numb.

"Okay, I'll see you then," she responded in her usual cheerful way.

As she closed the door, she gave Shand the same smile he remembered so well from before, the one that destroyed barriers.

Shand walked down the path with his stomach in his throat. He recounted the kiss over and over on the way back. It had definitely been longer than a usual cheek kiss, and softer too, or maybe he just imagined that it was. He could still feel her lips on his cheek and remember how her hair smelled when she was close.

Shand figured he should not give the intentions of the kiss too much thought or he would drive himself crazy. It was positive no matter what, and even though it wasn't a kiss on the lips, the more he thought about it, the more it seemed appropriate for who she was.

Shand spent the next few days trying to keep busy and not think about Bear. He stayed busy, but his mind stayed on Bear.

Shand returned to Bear's home on the third day...and every day after that.

Every morning, Shand would fish with Lain, then trade a portion of his catch for a choice piece of pork or lamb and vegetables. He would make it to Bear's just in time to prepare lunch. She would weave, and he would cook. They would share glances and smiles until the meal was ready, then sit next to each other and take their time to eat it. The afternoons were usually spent taking walks or lying under their favorite tree talking. Shand would jokingly ask what she thought their children might look like and when they would be married. She would giggle like he wasn't serious, but never discounted the notions.

Bear taught Shand to sew correctly, and Shand taught Bear to fish. They weren't getting much weaving done, but neither of them minded. Shand asked on a number of occasions about her name. But she would always say, "I'll tell you someday."

If Shand persisted, then she would retreat. So he let it go.

By summer, the weaving was complete, and Shand's sheet was finally tangible. It ended up being just over two horses square when fully expanded. Bear's tool only allowed her to make sections of fabric about a tenth the size of the completed sheet, and her dyeing bin was only large enough for one section to be dyed at a time, so the slight differences in each section of fabric, and the differences in the dye mixed for each section, resulted in an unexpected beauty—nine perfect squares, varying in hues of red, stitched together with bone-colored thread, then finished with beautifully-bound edges and precisely-bound holes, which Shand had instructed her to put along the top and bottom. It was like a work of art, and even better, a functional work of art.

Bear asked a number of times what the giant cloth was for, and Shand would always reply, "I'll show you someday. Maybe when you tell me about your name." Bear did not like that response and tried to coax the answer from him with sweetness, but Shand would never let it out.

Shand told Bear he needed to return to Lain's village for a while to work with the sheet, and if everything worked properly, he would have something great to show her.

He wrapped the sheet as tight as he could, then folded it in half and tied it to a makeshift sled that he had thrown together from the wood piles behind Bear's home.

As he tied the last of the knots, he felt Bear approach from behind and press her face against his back. She slid her arms between his ribs and elbows and pulled him in snug.

"You're coming back, right?" she asked.

The question surprised Shand. He thought his affection for her had been nauseatingly obvious.

"Of course. Don't be silly," Shand replied.

Shand turned and the two embraced for much longer than the typical departure hug.

Bear arched her back to look deep into Shand's eyes, then released him and stepped back. Neither said anything as Shand made a final check of the sled and knots. Bear stood with her arms folded and the majority of her weight on one leg. Shand smiled at her as he lifted the end of the sled. She smiled back, but only partially. He looked over his shoulder only once, just before rounding the bend. She had not moved and her partial smile was gone.

Shand dragged the sled down the overgrown path and into the haze of dusk. His thoughts were fixed on the sheet and his boat, compulsively going over every scenario possible for the construction of his new innovation. The sound from the sled dragging through the dirt seemed to get louder as the day grew darker, until he felt like it was all he could hear, possibly drowning out the steps of another person—or a predator. So he would frequently stop to listen. The forest would seem silent at first, but as his ears adjusted, the mosaic of sounds would slowly amplify and expand around him.

The steps of something heavy would have sounded much different than the common forest noises, and Shand did not have to remain still for long before feeling comfortable that he was alone. Still, his heart remained alert for the remainder of the walk, expecting to hear a presence every time he stopped.

Shand returned to Stone Man at the same time the Late-Nighters were gathering around their personal fire pit. The group was mostly composed of older men who liked to drink and tell stories, each storyteller trying to outdo the one before. Sometimes, when Shand felt restless, he would join the Nighters to listen to their tales and try to relax. The stories of warriors, beasts, and gods would paint images in Shand's mind that on occasion could calm the churning of obsessive thoughts he had for his boat, Bear, and anything else making his mind run.

The men of Stone Man were much different than the men in his village. They behaved like a pack, always together and wild. In Long Sky, the men were more individualistic, like each one was the chief of their own family-tribe. Each family-tribe was a piece of the larger village-tribe, headed by Chief Barra and his group of advising elders. The family leaders had an equal say in village decisions, no matter how big or small the family. When a large majority of the leaders were in agreement, Barra would usually rule in their favor. But in times of divisiveness, and of course with the ulterior-motivated advisement of the elders, it seemed the chief always ruled for the outcome that would produce the least resistance, which Shand thought would undoubtedly catch up with them some day.

It was all very organized, unlike the chain of command in Stone Man, or the lack thereof. Their village's decisions were made around the community fire pit in *majority wins* tradition. The entire village participated, women, the elderly, even the children. They would all gather around the pit at dusk. The children would prepare the fire, and the adult men would usually start the bickering. Everyone would slowly splinter off into groups until there were two distinct sides. If the two sides were nearly equal in number, the perceived spearhead from each side would give a speech to try and win converts, and if the speeches did not sway the vote, they would have a contest of bravery to expose the man who did not have total conviction—or at least that was how it was supposed to appear.

Shand realized early on that the spearhead for each side was merely a shill for the shadow leaders, and the entire procession was just a game played by a few—a game that involved a great deal of strategy and manipulation. The leaders had to pick a man sharp enough to articulate their ideas just in case the speech was the deciding factor, but dull enough not to catch wind of the game. However, winning the game at the speech level was rare, because the crowd always seemed to stay split intentionally after the speeches to guarantee a contest.

The chosen man also had to be willing to put himself in great danger to win the contest. This was where the most thought came in. Not only did he have to believe in the cause, he must have more conviction than the other side's shill, and preferably be more capable of winning. If the leaders ever had any doubts about their man, they would attempt to have the contest modified or changed to better suit him, which added another layer to the game, involving manipulation of the crowd to cheer for a specific contest suggestion.

The mob never had trouble coming up with bigger and more dangerous contests—the more dangerous or foolish the better. It seemed everyone was in silent agreement that the night was really about how far the madness could be pushed. Shand had witnessed everything from old men jumping out of trees to pain tolerance contests involving hot metal pokers. He had even watched two men hop around with tied hands for over an hour, trying to kick each other in the groin.

The ultimate win was to have your shill perceivably win the debate, but still have the night continue to the contest portion, only to have your man win again in the most dangerous and outrageous contest to date, resulting in your opinion becoming law—in conjunction with engineering the most exciting night in memory.

Shand thought their system was rather stupid, but it was far more fun to participate in than his village's process, and strangely, in the end, unlike his village, everyone would be in agreement, like the gods had chosen the outcome rather than the fools in the contest. In a way, Shand thought they did.

Shand figured he should skip the social with the Nighters in favor of a good night's sleep. He knew tomorrow would be a big day and wanted to be as sharp as possible. The Nighters ribbed him, as he'd expected, after their invitations to join them were kindly rejected.

"You need your sleep, little girl?" They teased.

"Bear lady not letting you play with your friends anymore?"

"What's on the sled? The body of the fun Shand?"

But Shand had one ready for them.

"It's tiring succeeding where so many have failed," Shand laughed. "I'll see you fools tomorrow night."

"Baaahhh! Booohhh!" The group bellowed.

Alby, the most boisterous of the group, pushed to the front of the men.

"She's just playing you! The Bear would never have a baby boy like you. She needs a man, like me!" he bellowed as he thrust his hips forward and smacked his thighs.

Shand pretended that none of the ribbing bothered him as he passed the group, smiling and making fart noises with his mouth, though he knew Alby's comment would rest in his mind for a good while.

When Shand arrived at his boat, he immediately retrieved the deck post and cross-poles from under the dock. He laced the sheet to the cross-poles, one pole to the top of the sheet, the other to the bottom, then slid the post into place just like before. He attached a large hook to the post near the top and one upside down near the bottom, both facing the bow.

Shand's hands began to sweat, and his heart started to race.

There was only a slight breeze, and he was unsure if it would be enough. Shand pushed off and began rowing out to sea, his excitement turning into unlimited fuel for the oars. Quickly making it over the surf, he pulled the oars in and positioned the rolled-up sheet in front of the deck post. He tied rope around the middle of the top cross-pole before running the end of the rope over the top hook on the post. As he pulled the other end of the rope, the sheet began to rise and unravel. As it rose, it came alive, knocking around in the breeze. It flopped and twisted, uncontrolled and powerful, like a tethered hawk.

Shand's ears began to tingle; the moment of truth had come. He quickly tied the middle of the bottom cross-pole to the bottom hook on the post, then tied control ropes to each end of the cross-poles, just like the giant leaf and its vines from his dream.

He grabbed the ends of the four control ropes, the two portside ropes in his left hand, starboard ropes in his right, then moved toward the stern until they were taut. Moving his arms back and forth, he changed the angles of the sheet, trying to catch the breeze. Slowly, back and forth, he let rope out and pulled rope in. Suddenly, the sheet filled tight with a *pop*, strongly tugging the boat forward.

'*You got it!*" said the voice in unison with Shand's thoughts.

But as quickly as Shand's heart filled with hope, it was replaced with frustration as the boat quickly lost the wind and was pulled off course. He tried to move the catcher as the boat moved to compensate, but it was hopeless. Over and over, he would catch the breeze only to be pulled from it. Finally, Shand dropped the ropes and flopped down to sulk.

His mind was frustrated and blank. He could not think. He could only feel the unique rush of the breeze pulling him across the water.

He had to catch it, to master it.

There was no longer a choice. The rush drained from his head to his heart, then pumped through his veins to touch every part of his body, finally settling deep in his guts where it sprouted roots.

He had to figure it out no matter what it took.

"The solution is simple, you fool. You use your paddles to keep your bow pointed in the direction you need, right? Why can't you do the same?"

Shand's mind sparked.

Images of steering the boat with the oars uncontrollably raced across his mind. He saw ropes between his teeth and tied to his feet, being tugged and pulled as he maneuvered the oars; images of ropes anchored to the deck, or in a slipknot around his wrist to be adjusted on the fly. But none of the images stuck in his mind, to be examined and tweaked. He felt like the breeze would find a way to escape his catcher no matter what. Maybe it was just over, and failure had already taken place.

"Why do you help me?" Yelled Shand. "First you give me advice, then you tell me I'm a demon! Then you try and help me again!"

"Hello? Haaaaaaahhhhhhhhh!"

"You pushed me out... The truth is, I do not know if you are a demon or not. I don't know anything about you, but I do know that you pushed me out. Do you have memories of childhood? I do. I remember when Baird was born and father dropped him, do you? Can you really tell me you feel the same as you did before father died?"

Shand remained silent, staring across the black water. The voice was right. He did not feel the same. But he did remember when father dropped Baird.

"Do you remember when my voice was inside, before the stress of the savages caused you to push me all the way out, and even before that, when our voices were almost equal, maybe just the two sides of a consciousness. The only way to find out is to let me back

in. If you or I are a demon then it will be evident. The demon can move on to find its way, and Shand can move on with no pestering voice, and if we are a split entity, we can become whole again."

Shand sat quietly. Thoughts clouded his mind like never before.

He did not respond. He had too much to think about. But he did know one thing: he was in control, no matter what the truth was, and he wanted to remain that way.

Shand slowly unhooked the catcher from the deck post. He felt a calmness as he rolled the sheet. He moved slowly and felt lighter than usual. As he broke everything down, a feeling of patience fell over him. He knew that somehow his idea would work, just maybe not like he had thought.

On his way back, the images continued to cross his mind. He let them come freely, to move in and out of his head as though on a breeze. Some images circled back to come together with others, forming pictures that seemed to have spirits of their own; Shand could not control them, even if he had wanted to. The flat translucent images flew around, turning and tossing like leaves in the wind, then floated down and stacked on top of each other, creating a new three-dimensional image. But as the layers stacked, the image grew darker. He only had a second to record the near-completed image before it faded to black.

His condition remained acute even after making it back to the dock and crawling into the hull to lie down. When he closed his eyes, the images became clearer and even more independent, like he was in a waking dream.

Over the next two days, Shand worked slowly and precisely. He felt aged and patient as he forged and carved the steering assembly. He took bits and pieces from the images he had seen and put them to practice in his imagination, coming up with what he thought would be the simplest and most effective design.

Shand made longer cross-pole control ropes to reach the bench seat near the new steering wing at the stern. He tied knots near the ends of the ropes about thirty centimeters apart. He then anchored two fasteners on either side of the bench. The fasteners were like hooks, open on one side and just large enough to slip the rope in and out. The knots existed to stop the rope from sliding through the hooks and to hold the sheet in a chosen position.

After everything was set and tight, when Shand could think of nothing more to do, he closed his eyes and waited for night. There was no anxiousness, no restlessness. His heartbeat was slow and soft. He was unsure if he fell asleep, but the next time he opened his eyes it was dark and the moon was high.

Shand set out the same as before. The breeze was stronger and colder than on his first run. He rowed to his familiar spot and got ready. This time, he hooked the four cross-pole control ropes to the fasteners near the bench seat first, leaving moderate slack, and then raised the catcher.

Returning to the bench, he sat to the right of the steering wing handle, grabbing the handle with his left hand, then unfastened the two cross-pole ropes on his right side, holding them tight in his right hand. Shand slowly pulled the ropes in until the angle was just right and the catcher tried to fill. He quickly anchored those two ropes in the hooks, then scooted to the left side of the wing, grabbing the wing's handle with his right hand. He then released the two ropes on his left side to hold with his left hand.

He pulled the ropes in to feel them pull back and try to fishtail the boat off course. But this time Shand could steer, and he kept the boat angled so the catcher stayed full. Pulling the ropes tight, Shand gained speed. The boat tilted higher and higher as waves crashed against the hull. Faster and faster he skipped over the waves until he was racing across the water like riding a horse in a dead run. The harder he pulled the ropes, the faster he went and the more the boat tilted. If he let the ropes out, then he slowed and the tilt reduced.

Shand had never had so much fun. He raced back and forth along the coast, seeing how fast he could go, and how far he could tilt the vessel without capsizing. It was a feeling unlike any Shand had ever experienced. A clean exhilaration. Effortless. Propelled by a force that would never tire.

He had done it.

He had caught the wind.

CHAPTER V

The Return

Shand could not wait to show Royce his invention. At the speeds he could now reach, it should only take him a few days to make it back to Long Sky. Royce could experience the catcher and Shand could be back just before Bear started to worry. He could even bring Royce with him to meet her.

Shand pulled the ropes tight and headed north. He watched the lights of Stone Man quickly fade into the night and thought he might even make it back quicker than he first anticipated. His mind and eyes were wide-awake, and there was no fatigue in his back or joints. He swelled with an energy he thought came straight from the gods.

He ran at full tilt through the night. No longer did he have to pull his rig slowly through the water with oars, powered only by his back and arms. Now there was no rowing or paddling, just riding. A group of dolphins accompanied him for a while; shooting back and forth in front of the bow and running up from behind to take a good look at him. He only had a few pieces of fish to offer them for the escort. He wished he had more to keep them around, but he barely had enough for himself. One dolphin remained after the others had gone. It seemed a little darker and larger than the others, and its dorsal fin was heavily scarred. It stayed near the stern just outside the steering wing, cutting back and forth, always keeping one of its eyes on Shand. Shand tried to call to the dolphin, mimicking its high-pitched chirps in hopes he might get a response. But the lone dolphin never made a sound. It gave one last long look at Shand, then disappeared under the black water, once again leaving Shand with only his thoughts to keep him company.

When the horizon began to lighten, Shand slacked the ropes a bit to watch the sunrise at a calm speed. His body was tired from its high, and he thought it best to have a short sleep. He knew he would sleep deeply and he would awaken refreshed, ready for a day of full-tilt running, so he came a little closer to the shore, lowered the sheet and tossed an anchor, then crawled into the hull and curled up with his blanket.

The next time his eyes opened, it was afternoon. Shand jumped from the hull, half asleep, with weak legs and blurry eyes. He scanned the shoreline and sea, almost seeing little blonde demons swimming to his boat with his half-dreaming mind.

Shand hurried to raise the catcher. His good sleep had put him behind schedule. He began to wonder about Bear and imagined the look on her face if she thought he wasn't coming back.

Shand pulled the sheet tight. His eyes were wide, his body alert. He ran all day and into the night, not stopping to eat or rest. The beaches were slowly transforming back into rock and boulders. He knew he was getting close, so he decided to push through the night.

Just before sunrise, Shand recognized his first landmark—a giant stone finger, topped with a disc-like boulder. It was the farthest point he had been before the expedition. He wanted to show Royce the catcher as a surprise before unveiling it to the village, so he let the ropes out and began dismantling his wind catcher. The row from the finger to Long Sky would be grueling, but he did not want to risk being seen by the fisherman.

He arrived at the Long Sky dock just as the fishermen were returning from the morning run. They quickly crowded around Shand's boat.

"How far did you go?" one questioned.

"What have you brought back?" another one asked.

Shand felt silly that he had nothing to show them.

"I did find treasure, but it was stolen by cannibals." Shand smiled.

He felt like one of the old men in Stone Man, telling inflated stories that could never be proven.

"Sure it was!" Royce's voice rumbled as he pushed himself through the crowd.

Shand didn't realize how much he had missed his uncle until he saw him. He had to hold back tears, trying to compose himself in a strong hug.

"You didn't die!" Royce snickered. "Thank the gods."

"You wouldn't believe how many times I almost did."

Shand announced to the group that he would tell everyone about his journey that evening around the main fire pit, joking that he only had the energy to tell the story once. Royce, of course, stayed on the boat with Shand after the fisherman dispersed.

"You have something more to tell, don't you," Royce declared. "It's written all over your face."

"Yes." Shand smiled. "And it's incredible."

Royce slowly lowered his large frame to sit on the boat's edge. "We'll, let's hear it."

Shand momentarily considered hoisting the deck post and showing Royce right then, but he wanted to show him when it was just the two of them and they could have the sea to themselves.

"I will show you tonight. After I tell the village about the journey."

Royce raised a bushy orange eyebrow in disappointment. "That's fine," he muttered. "But you're going to tell me about the journey now…right?"

Telling Royce the story didn't really count on the annoying-retold-story list. He was the only one that would truly identify with Shand's perspective during all that had happened.

Royce wore a constant smile as Shand told him how he had been hunted in the forest, how he dodged spears and ran like a fool through the woods. Shand proudly told him how he had outsmarted the native, how the native tried to summon spirits to kill him, and how he rescued his stolen boat and escaped, only to be hunted down again.

Shand had to backtrack in the story a little; he had started where he thought Royce would be the most interested, forgetting about the treasure and the dying woman. He watched Royce's face carefully as he told him about the rich woman and what he had done to her, hoping Royce's expression would reflect approval; but, as usual, his face was difficult to read.

They talked for hours. Royce told Shand how Baird was getting out of control, and how Shand's name was already being used in conversation the same way the names of notable villagers from the past were used. Sometimes in discussions in Shand's favor; others not so much. He explained that most of the villagers had expected him to return within a week, and when he did not, they had to modify their opinions to stay in the right.

"He probably capsized and drowned," some had said.

"He must have been ill-prepared and starved," said others.

"Some thought you might have found a better land inhabited by primitive people you could rule, like Cesan the Ancient. I figured you'd be back around now," Royce smirked, standing up to put his giant hand on Shand's shoulder. "Come have some stew. I know a good boy that would love to see you."

Shand couldn't believe he had let Thief slip his mind. "Yes! Yes! That sounds great," he replied.

Shand pushed their pace down the path. He could not wait to see Thief and scratch him into submission. Royce told Shand he should stay with him for the night, and that he had been letting Thief sleep inside.

"I'm not sure Thief would accept sleeping on a dirty, cold boat now. He has gotten pretty used to what I have set up for him." Royce chuckled.

Shand followed Royce through the doorway to see Thief stretched out on a hay-filled bed almost as big as Royce's, lying next to the fireplace where Shand used to have slept.

"What have you done to my dog?" Shand said. "I hope you haven't removed all the *dog* from him."

Thief barely moved when the door was opened. He just cut his eyes to check the presence from under an upside-down head. But when he heard Shand's voice, he flipped over in one quick motion. Shand jumped down on the bed, rigorously scratching the lazy beast. Thief whimpered, licking Shand's face and neck. Thief did not smell the same. Less like a dog and more like one of Bear's flower arrangements.

"Does this worthless dog ever go outside?" Shand asked. "He smells like he just got out of a hot bath sprinkled with scented oils."

"Well, if he's going to stay in my house, he surely can't smell like a dog, can he?"

Shand was a bit shocked, but he was happy Royce and Thief were taking good care of each another.

"It helps with the shedding too," said Royce, with an almost defensive tone.

Shand just giggled, causing a smile to creep onto Royce's face.

Thief and Shand rolled around, stretching and scratching on his bed, while Royce heated a stew. After Royce washed and changed clothes, he returned to find Shand and Thief fast asleep.

At dusk, Royce shook Shand's foot to wake him up. "You have a gathering to attend."

Shand stretched and rubbed his face against Thief's.

"Are you coming?" Shand asked Royce.

106

"No, I've heard the story, but I will definitely meet you afterward to hear your big news."

As Thief and Shand made their way to the fire pit, Shand's steps hastened in excitement to see his family. A crowd had already started to form in the large, open sided hut his village used for ceremonies and politics. He saw Duncan and Alroy paired off near the firewood pile, surely talking about old times. As soon as Baird saw Shand, the little monster tore down the path, kicking up dust and almost stumbling over his feet; he clumsily jumped into Shand's arms, heavier than both anticipated. He saw Banan smiling and waving with Filib resting on her hip as usual.

"Where are Mother and Catrin?" Shand asked Banan.

"They will be here soon. They waited to finish cooking the lamb and bring all the food at once."

Shand's stomach growled uncontrollably. Ana's lamb was his favorite. He gave proper hellos to Alroy and Duncan, then sat on his usual stump near the fire to wait on Ana and Catrin and any straggling villagers. The villagers surrounded him, asking questions that he answered with vague, short answers.

"I will tell the whole story when my family gets here, and we can all have a bite around the fire."

Some villagers gave snide looks or rolled their eyes to his response, while others didn't seem to care either way and just looked happy to be there and eat free food.

Ana was not smiling when she and Shand first made eye contact. It looked like she was scanning Shand's face and body for abnormalities. She put the food down on the long wood table that had been a centerpiece of the village since Shand could remember. She embraced Shand strongly, rubbing her hands up and down his back and over his arms like she was feeling for hidden injuries.

"I'm fine, Mother," Shand said. "Strong and healthy."

Ana's posture relaxed, and she gave him kisses on both cheeks while Catrin hugged his back.

Shand's throat tightened. He began to think his heart was softer than he had thought. He was more than happy to be home and almost as happy to eat Ana's lamb.

Shand decided to begin his tale with a question from a young boy: "Did you discover any new lands?"

"Yes, I did," Shand said, projecting his voice into the crowd. "And the cannibals from the stories are true! I saw them, and they look much different than you imagine."

The smacking of lips and chattering conversations became almost silent as Shand continued his story of the tiny savages and their sun-colored, bowl-shaped hair and milky skin.

The children's faces did not move. Their mouths hung open and their expressions were blank, the best proof that he was telling the tale well. Maybe he *had* learned something from the old men in Stone Man. Half of the adult faces looked unsure, some wrinkling their foreheads, others raising eyebrows. But Shand could tell that even the adults were giving him their complete attention. He left Bear out of the tale. He didn't think anyone wanted to hear about that, and he didn't want to be harassed by his sisters and mother afterwards. He ended the tale in the same place he had with Lain. It was really the only decent climax.

He spent the remainder of the night sitting in a small circle, just his family, next to the fire. Baird sat in Shand's lap, or really, halfway laid in his lap with his feet stretched out and unsettled. Filib took turns curling up in the laps of Banan, Catrin and Ana. They talked about Alroy and how old and disconnected he was, and how bad Baird's behavior had become. Shand was sure they were hinting responsibility for Baird's behavior towards him, and really, they had every right to, he thought. He just didn't like the way they were doing it.

"Two strong sisters and an incredible mother couldn't tame the savage Baird beast for a few months? I don't believe that," Shand said.

There was no response from the group, just looks that only sisters can give. Shand was unsure why he had even said that. Maybe to help with the heavy guilt he felt for leaving the family so shortly after their father's death, leaving Baird with no strong male guidance. Alroy didn't really count. He was a good provider, but he had no patience with children and no tolerance for being bothered. Alroy already put himself on a pedestal for taking care of his dead son's family, and any additional sacrifice would just be silly. He was far too busy ensuring his stature within the community and socializing with the elder men to waste his time on a spoiled little brat, especially since the brat's sisters—who had caused the problem in the first place—would only undo his work.

"I'm sorry," Shand said. "I will be around a lot more now." Shand gripped Baird under his arms and slid him up to sit in his lap. "And you and I are going hunting, and fishing, and I might even take you on a ride down the Escaping River," he added in his beast voice with a bit of a rib tickle for Baird, bringing a smile to everyone's face, especially Ana's.

Shand's family members were the only ones left around the fire when Royce walked out of the shadows.

109

"I need to steal Shand from you. We have business to discuss," Royce said in his matter-of-fact tone. Everyone stretched and yawned, slowly rising to give Shand hugs.

"I will see you in the morning for breakfast," Ana reminded.

"Yes, yes, I remember. I will be there."

"Bet I can eat more than you now!" Declared Baird.

"Guess we'll find out in the morning… But if there is pork…you lose," replied Shand.

As Shand led Royce and Thief down the rocky path towards the dock, nothing was said. Shand felt at home hearing the almost-hypnotizing sounds of the pebbles beneath their feet as their steps moved in and out of cadence. He had nearly forgotten.

Royce didn't mention the bronze sleeve in the middle of the deck as they boarded, and he said nothing as Shand fished out the deck post from under the dock. He remained still, sitting on the edge as Shand laid the post on the deck with its end sticking off the stern. Thief took his position at the tip of the bow to intercept any sea monsters on the attack.

Shand kicked the boat away from the dock and fastened the oars. He rowed over the surf and continued until he thought they were out of the village's sight. He raised the post and began wriggling it in place. Royce sat quietly, not asking if help was needed, nor what Shand was doing. He just watched, relaxed and expressionless. As Shand hoisted the catcher, it knocked around as usual, forcing Royce to move position. Royce landed near the stern, catching a glimpse of the wing. Shand could see Royce's wheels turning and that made Shand even more excited.

When things were in place, Shand accompanied Royce at the stern, two control ropes in hand. He grabbed the wing's handle, and with a few minor adjustments, the sheet filled with air. The breeze was strong and the initial tug was the best so far, causing Royce to brace himself and Thief to dig his nails into the deck. Royce separated his hands farther along the boat's edge for more stability. Thief quickly took a more secure position across Shand's lap.

As they picked up speed, Shand sneaked glances at Royce, waiting for his astonished approval. But Royce just looked ahead like it was his hundredth wind-powered trip. Shand had to get up to full speed and a good tilt before he got a reaction—laughter. Royce laughed like Shand had never heard. A good and deep belly laugh as they bounced along. He even let out a "whoooo" a few times.

Shand had even more fun than on his virgin run. Thief, not so much. The action was too much to handle in conjunction with protecting the pack. After running up and down the coast for a while, Royce leaned over and shouted through the wind, "You're going to let me drive, right?"

Shand slacked the ropes "Of course, of course, sorry... Isn't it incredible?"

"Of course it is. It's the most incredible thing I have ever seen." Royce laughed

They took turns coming up with all the things they could do now, becoming louder and more excited with every suggestion.

"We can hunt animals no one has ever seen!"

"We can travel farther in one day than we could in a month before!"

"We can go to where the world ends!"

"We can find new and better fishing spots with incredible new fish, and become the wealthiest fishermen in history!"

Shand watched Royce's face light up brighter than ever as Royce pulled the ropes and tried to get the steering wing in just the right position to achieve maximum speed. They laughed in excitement as Royce let the ropes out just before capsizing.

At this point, Thief had had enough and was whining for a return, or at least a slowdown.

"Okay, okay…we'll take it easy, boy," said Royce as he slacked the ropes. "Who knows about this invention?"

"No one. Just you and me."

Royce rested his back, leaning over to put his forearms on his knees. He looked into the distance like he was watching his thoughts on the horizon.

"The more I think about it, the more I think you need to give a lot of thought to whom you share this knowledge with, and what the effects could be," Royce said.

Shand did not respond. He thought about what Royce said as he dismantled the catcher. He began to feel that Royce had selfish intentions for keeping the catcher a secret. Shand did not want to believe that about his uncle, but his mind kept returning to the idea.

Royce took the oars to row back as silent payback for Shand's prior row. Shand could see that Royce was watching him, and he tried to be neutral with his demeanor. Neither said a word for the remainder of the trip.

Just before the beach came into focus, Thief gave out a single strong bark at the shore. Shand and Royce squinted into to the distance to see a figure standing on the dock. They gave each other the look they gave when no words were needed.

Royce continued to row. They both remained silent as the figure's white hair, which reflected the moonlight, became clear. It was Alroy, standing on the dock with his arms folded like he had just caught them sneaking out.

"Guess you didn't go as far out as you thought," Alroy snickered.

Royce and Shand remained silent. No nods or even grunts.

"I saw you in the moonlight," Alroy said. "No need to hide anything. It was the most amazing thing I have seen."

"I was just telling Shand how we might need to keep this a secret…Guess it's too late for that." Royce laughed.

"Well," Alroy said, reaching down to help them out of the boat. "I'm glad you said that. Because I agree with you… As I watched you skip across the sea, all I could envision was the access this innovation would create."

"Access?" Shand irritably grunted. Alroy had a habit of speaking in riddles when he thought he knew something others did not, and that grated on Shand's nerves.

"Yes, access…access to better fishing, better hunting…and access to the world."

"Yep, that's what I'm thinking," replied Shand.

"But have you thought about the access for others? As I watched you and the speeds you were achieving, I began to see the ocean filled with these types of vessels…and those vessels filled with foreign warriors."

Royce did not say a word. He just watched Shand's face, like a father watching how his son handles getting knocked down. Shand felt stupid and childish. He sat quietly. He had never even considered the knowledge moving beyond his village. He had been focused only on the mechanics of the invention and how it could improve their lives.

"We must give this serious thought," said Alroy. "Between the three of us, we can figure out how to use this innovation to best serve our tribe."

Royce slowly bobbed his head in agreement. He put his arm around Shand and gripped his shoulder. "Don't look sad, boy! You've made something incredible. We just need a plan."

"Let us have drinks at Royce's and discuss the future," announced Alroy.

Alroy, Royce, Shand, and Thief, in that order, walked in a single-file line and in silence down the path to Royce's home. When Thief realized the destination, he took the lead, watching the forest closely for predators, and stopping to listen every so often in case the predators were well hidden.

They sat around Royce's table for hours, discussing all the scenarios they could think of. Of course, Alroy did most of the talking, given that he thought his words carried the most weight. Royce did not say much, mainly nodding in agreement as Shand prophesied about the unforeseen positive effects and additional innovation that could come from setting the new knowledge free in the village. Royce would also nod with Alroy and his general theme of "safety first."

The night ended with an agreement that they should at least keep it amongst themselves until they felt comfortable about the next move. Alroy said they could give it more thought, and in the meantime, they could take secret voyages to better understand where their village was in the world and where large and possible hostile tribes might be located.

Royce had the idea of leading a land expedition while Alroy and Shand could take to the sea. Each expedition could create maps, and, on their return, combine the maps into an unprecedented knowledge of the world.

Shand figured there was no way he was getting trapped on a boat with Alroy for any length of time, and that he had other, more important things in his future than being controlled by an old man, namely, Bear and his own exploration.

"Well, let's just think about it." Shand yawned.

"Yes, it's late, and we could have a clearer discussion fully rested," declared Alroy.

Thief was fast asleep on his custom bed, so Shand decided not to disturb him. He gave Royce and Alroy firm forearm shakes, then headed out.

Just as Shand was about to take the path to the dock, Alroy called to him from Royce's stoop. "Hey, boy! I forgot to ask you... How did you come up with the sheet?"

Shand was tired and did not fully turn around. "It was a vision," he replied.

Alroy did not respond. Shand turned to see Alroy staring at him. Alroy began walking towards him. He cleared his throat and said, "A vision?"

"Yes," Shand flatly replied.

"Let me walk with you, and you can tell me about this vision."

Shand headed down the path at a pace of his choosing. He was saturated with Alroy's presence and ready for bed.

"It came to me in my sleep after the exhausting battle with the natives at sea, in the form of a leaf I had seen earlier that day."

"Fascinating," replied Alroy. "Let me ask you another question. Do you remember when you were a child and I taught you to skin a rabbit?"

Shand paused. He could not figure out why Alroy had asked him such a question.

"Yes, I remember," Shand shortly replied. "Why? What does that have to do with anything?"

"What was the color of the rabbit's eyes?" Alroy asked.

Shand remembered the rabbit's eye color well because one eye had been blue and the other brown. But Shand did not answer. He felt like Alroy was setting him up for something, and he did not want to play along.

"*RUN!*"

The voice shocked him. He quickly turned to look at Alroy's face just before seeing a flash, followed by a solid blow that rang out in Shand's head as everything went black.

Shand could hear his head pounding before he could open his eyes. He could feel his hands tied behind his back. He was on the floor with his back against a wall. His head hung low and his mouth was full of something. His eyes slowly opened to the blurry sight of the inside of

Alroy's cottage. Alroy was sitting in a chair facing Shand with his legs crossed and a drink in his hand. In his other hand, he held a long wooden rod.

"You should have run."

"I'm going to remove the cloth from your mouth, but only if you give me your word you will not cry out… If you do, I will not stop striking until you are unconscious… Do you understand?"

Shand slowly nodded his head. Alroy reached his old fingers in Shand's mouth and pulled out a dirty piece of cloth.

"So…what was the color of the rabbit's eyes?"

"Answer him, but say nothing else. He is an evil man. I cannot explain right now; just do exactly what I say."

Shand swallowed and tried to regain some clarity.

"Blue and brown," he replied.

"Good, that's correct, my boy… But I still have some questions for you to make sure."

"To make sure of what?" said Shand.

"To make sure you are who you say you are."

"Do you hear a voice?" asked Alroy.

"Say no. He will kill you."

Shand remained silent. His mind was racing and he could not slow it down. He felt silence was his best option.

"Is the voice talking to you now? Let me guess. The voice has told you not to speak. And you would listen to a voice over a family member because why? …Let me make another guess… The voice told you it was the real Shand and that you were a lost demon, right? And that you needed to let him back in to make sure."

Shand mind went flat. How did he know this? Maybe Alroy *could* save him.

"He killed your father and now he's going to kill you."

"Its name is Orr, and it said the same thing to me and your father. It attached to me many years ago, but I was too strong willed for it, so it attached to your father."

"It just told me you killed my father," Shand said.

"Ahhh, you are in there, Orr." Alroy grinned. "So we meet again." Alroy raised his voice. "I was too strong willed for you, wasn't I, Orr? You had to move on to weaker prey, didn't you? On to my free spirited son, you cowardly little leech! Shand, Orr killed your father, and now he has moved on to you. But he made a mistake…because you are strong like me."

"He is lying to you. He gave no thought to your father's life and viewed him as weak. Alroy tried to expel me on his own, without the help of the healers. To keep the embarrassment of his son's possession a secret. He burned and tortured you father until he died. Yes, it is true I am a lost spirit. But I am not an evil spirit. Simply a spirit who has never lived. I only wish to have life. To feel what you feel. I would never steal someone's body forever. I just want to feel life. I would return the vessel before any real time had passed."

"I thought my father died in a fishing accident," Shand said to Royce.

"No, my boy. Orr caused his death because he would not release him."

"And you had to pretend he died at sea because his body was too damaged to be seen? And you did not tell the healers?" asked Shand.

"I know it is hard for you to understand, but I also believe you are wise enough to know how things truly work. Your father came to me soon after he first heard

118

Orr's voice…because he trusted me. He told me a spirit had begun talking to him and showed him the plank boat in a vision. We decided to create the story about seeing a plank boat at sea to ensure that your father's name would stay clear of discussions of visions and magic. It was your father's choice not to use the healers. He did not want anyone to know he heard a voice. When you told me about your vision, I knew I must have made a mistake and let Orr escape.

"The healers tell me a demon like Orr cannot survive for more than a few minutes on its own. It must have a human host. The healers protect themselves and the room with the smoke of the Calet root during the ritual, so the demon cannot attach to them or escape the room. Once expelled by pain and ancient verse, the demon is said to return to the underworld in a scream that is only felt, not heard."

"He is the evil one, not me. He hated your father and all his silly dreaming and philosophizing. He lost sleep at night over the embarrassment he felt. Have I not helped you? Have I not shown you great things? What has he done for you except kill your father?"

"I performed the ritual on your father at sea to ensure it stayed a secret, and to minimize the chance of escape. But I must have made a mistake in protecting myself. Orr must have detached from your father during the ritual and attached to me, then attached to you after I returned. That is why the ritual went too far. Orr tricked me. It's the cause of your father's death.

I believe Orr is a powerful demon with knowledge far past our imagination, and maybe it can't help but leak some of this knowledge while trying to possess a body, or maybe the visions are intentional in some way I don't understand. Images have to come to me at night of Orr standing at the bow of a large boat, looking at me through the eyes of its human host, and behind it, thousands of plank boats filled with his demon-possessed warriors on their way to conquer all of man."

"Escape from these bindings, and I will show you who is evil. Strike him heavy and make him weak. I will transfer to him, and you will be free from me forever. I give you my word. You will have vengeance for your father, and I will have life."

"This time, I will not make a mistake. We will do everything perfectly, and you, I, and our entire family will be rid of Orr forever."

Shand wiped his nose on his shoulder. As he attempted to adjust his eye patch with his shoulder, he caught a glimpse of a black nose peeking out from behind Alroy's rear door. The beautiful nose of his best friend. It did not move. It just sniffed, staying just far enough outside to ensure the door would not creak.

Smartest dog in the world, Shand thought.

Shand quickly kicked his feet and rustled. "Git! Git!" he called.

Alroy immediately stood up to strike Shand with the rod. But Thief was already in stride. He launched himself over a chair to sink his teeth deep into Alroy's forearm just as the rod made contact with Shand's neck.

Thief did not release to bite again. He kept his jaws gripped, thrashing back and forth, trying to rip Alroy's arm apart. Alroy could not resist. He could only give slack.

Shand quickly wriggled the binding under his butt and over his legs. He jumped on Alroy's back, locking his ankles around Alroy's waist. Being pulled and tugged by Thief, Alroy could not stop Shand from getting his wrist bindings over Alroy's head and around his neck.

Shand leaned back, anchoring his elbows in the center of Alroy's back, pulling the bindings back, deeper and deeper into Alroy's neck.

Alroy fell to the floor like a well-speared deer. Thief released his arm, then immediately began checking Shand's condition with licks and sniffs.

"Tie his hands and feet. Little Man is sitting on the table. Take it and strike him in thick meat. Not enough to kill, but severely weaken. Then soak cloth with water and fill his mouth and nose with it. That will weaken him enough for me to get all the way inside... Trust me... I will be forever indebted to you."

Shand retrieved Little Man from the table. He tied Alroy's feet and hands together, then rolled him onto his back.

"Not too deep."

Little man punched into Alroy's chest muscle like he was a pig—heavy and solid.

Shand followed with two quick hacks, one to each side of the neck in thick muscle. Then two more, one for each thigh.

After his mouth and nose had been filled with the soaked cloth, Alroy began to move. He coughed and sucked the cloth like he was drowning. Alroy panicked; he tried to pull his hands out of the binding like he was trying to rip off his arms. But his lack of air caused the frenzy to quickly suck away what strength he had.

Shand could feel the voice rise from his body.

Little by little, Alroy's coughing and convulsing slowed. His movements turned to those of a rodent's last breaths.

121

Shand could almost see Orr entering Alroy's body. Alroy's body became calm. The panic turned to rest. His eyes closed and his face relaxed. It looked like he was almost grinning. Then his face turned to look at Shand with new eyes—wider and deeper. Shand waited a minute, then removed the cloth and cut the bindings.

"Thank you my friend," Alroy's mouth said with a new, flat inflection. "You will not be sorry... But I need one last favor from you. The damage you inflicted on this body was greater than I thought, and I can hardly move. Please, dress my wounds. You can leave me where I lay. I just need to ensure this body does not die. I am sure I will be strong enough to make my way in a day or so; then, I promise, you will never see or hear from me again."

Shand nodded.

He looked through Alroy's things in search of proper cloth. Orr lay on the ground, staring at the ceiling, smiling. Thief came over every so often to give Orr a good sniff and look at Shand for approval. When Shand returned with cloth and water, Orr was asleep. Shand did not clean or dress any wounds. He told Thief to stay and walked out the front door.

As Shand hurried down the path, he saw two figures walking towards him.

"You were just the ones I was coming to find!" said Shand.

It was Dorces and Faitin, the village's healers. The two men looked surprised. They just stood and stared at Shand.

"Let me guess, my uncle came to you earlier tonight and said a ritual needs to be performed on me, right?"

They remained silent, glancing down at Shand's bloody axe sticking out from his waistband. "Please, hurry, come with me. There has been a change of plans. I will explain on the way."

Thief's ears perked at the creak of the door. He watched Shand's face slowly peek from behind the door and give Thief the quiet signal. He then watched two old men creep in behind Shand holding smoking roots in their hands.

They tiptoed around the entire cottage, blowing the smoke all over the walls and themselves. Then Dorces grabbed Orr's left arm, Faitin his right, and Shand pressed down on both ankles with all his weight.

Orr's eyes quickly opened. He said nothing. His wide eyes bounced back and forth among the three intruders.

"What is your name?" Dorces exclaimed.

"Alroy! Alroy!" Orr replied.

"What is the name of my second daughter?"

"What? Let me go. I don't need to remember such things."

"What is the name of my wife?" Dorces yelled.

Orr remained silent. He stared at Shand with eyes that would frighten even Royce.

"You will be sorry, you fool," Orr whispered.

Orr kicked and spit as the healers spoke verses and burned him with the roots.

He screamed in a language Shand did not understand as they forced biting insects into his mouth. The deep cuts in the chest and shoulders had no effect on the lengths to which Orr could push Alroy's body.

"If this goes on much longer, Alroy will not survive. His body may be already too weak," Faitin said.

"Don't stop," said Shand. "Alroy told me it's a powerful demon that has been haunting our people for years, and that he would never stand in the way of ridding our community of this disease."

Alroy stopped breathing before Orr began to release. Shand could sense the hatred Orr had for Alroy. Orr held Alroy's body arched and stiff, like he was torturing him as much as he could before he was expelled.

The healers were right. There was no mistaking it. You could feel the despair reaching out as the demon was sucked back into the dark. Back into a void Shand caught a glimpse of just before Orr went quiet, a place too dark too imagine—another memory Shand would try to forget.

Like so many before, Alroy did not survive the ritual. His body lay cold and still on the floor. Shand slowly looked over his body, making sure there was no life hiding in his chest or just behind his eyes. He ran his finger along the wound on Alroy's chest, before pulling his clothes back together to cover the injury.

Shand began poking around Alroy's home. He picked up anything he thought his siblings might want and wrapped them in a cloth. The healers told Shand they would prepare Alroy's body for the funeral, and that he should go home to rest.

Shand slept curled around Thief that night. He slept long and sound. No strange visions, just dreams, colorful and vivid images of the future, dreams of Bear and their children, dreams of distant exploration and discovery.

Shand was sitting on the dock with his feet hanging off the edge when Royce arrived for the morning fishing run.

"Have you come to accompany me fishing, like old times?" Royce asked.

"No. I have come to ask you to accompany me."

Royce paused and sprouted a smile across his cheeks. "Absolutely," he replied.

Shand retrieved the deck post from under the dock and laid it along the deck like before. Royce manned the ropes, and Shand got the oars in position just like their old routine. Royce took a seat at the rear and got comfortable as Shand began the row over the surf.

"So...where are we going?" Royce asked.

Shand paused and cracked a smile. "We are going to meet Bear."

Royce smiled even bigger. "We are going to meet a bear?"

THE END

60636842R00080

Made in the USA
Lexington, KY
13 February 2017